CHAPTER 1

I T WAS PANCAKE TUESDAY. The children sat round the kitchen table in their grandmother's house. They often came to their grandmother because their own home was not far away but this was the first time they were going to sleep there. They were going to stay till Easter. They felt a bit strange. The little boy, Mark, held his knife and fork ready. His elder sister, Hannah, told him to put them down and wait politely. His big brother told her to leave him alone.

'If Mammy was here, Ben, she would not let him behave like that,' Hannah said.

'She would so,' Ben answered, laughing, and he put his arm around Mark's shoulders.

Granny opened the back door and lifted in her griddle. It was heavy black iron. She settled it on top of the cooker.

'Reach me down my bowl of batter, Hannah,' she said, and Hannah went to the counter to lift the bowl. She had always loved that bowl with the picture of two cocks facing each other. There was a chip on one side where the children's father had dropped a ladle on it when he was fifteen.

'How did you make the batter, Granny?' Hannah asked politely.

'I made it before you arrived this afternoon,' Granny said, rubbing the griddle with a buttery paper. 'I put in three cups of flour for three children, three eggs, a lot of milk and a little salt.' She poured the batter from the bowl

3

into a big jug, and from the jug into three circles on the griddle. She waited, Hannah beside her, watching them.

'No good,' she said. 'The griddle is not hot enough yet. See, there are no bubbles rising. We'll have to wait.'

The children smiled at her. She put a bowl of fine sugar beside the cooker and a lemon cut in half. On the table, Hannah had set jam and honey for Mark. Granny turned the pancakes with her cooking knife. They were cooked in a kind of way but white on both sides. She put them on a plate and threw them out in the garden for the birds.

Then Granny was very busy because the griddle was ready. She rubbed butter on the hot black surface. She poured on batter and it sizzled. She flipped the pancake with her knife when she saw little bubbles rise. She lifted it to a heated plate, spread butter, lemon juice and sugar and rolled it up. She did that over and over again. Sometimes she put on just butter and served Mark while Hannah spread his jam or honey, whichever he chose. As quickly as Granny could serve the pancakes they were eaten.

'Keep some for yourself, Granny,' Ben said, so that Granny would not think that Hannah was the only one with manners.

'I'll just have a cup of tea,' Granny smiled. She lifted the hot griddle and leaned it against the wall outside the back door. The white pancakes lay like three little moons on the grass.

In the warm kitchen the plates were empty and the children were full. Their cheeks were shining. Their fingers were sticky. They sighed their satisfaction.

'What is Mammy doing now, do you think?' Hannah asked.

'I think she has just come out of that college she has flown to in Bristol,' Granny said. 'It's the first day of her course but even so, she has made friends with other people, some Irish like us, some English, some Scots.'

'And Welsh,' Ben said. 'Because Bristol isn't very far from Wales.'

'Certainly not as far as from Belfast,' Granny agreed. 'She has a big notebook and her umbrella. She stands at the top of some steps for a minute and two people say to her, "Come on, Alice, into town. We'll see can we get some pancakes." '

The children laughed. 'They won't be as good as your pancakes, Granny,' Hannah said.

'They will not,' Granny agreed. 'Then before she goes to bed tonight she will phone your Daddy in London to tell him how well she is doing.'

'Will she ring here?' Mark asked. 'Can I talk to her?'

'No,' Granny said. 'She will ring in a day or two to talk to you. That was what we agreed.'

When Hannah went to bed in the small room where her father had slept as a boy, she found it hard to settle in the strange place. So she closed her eyes and pictured, as she often did, a pink balloon tied to her gate at home, straining on a straight string to fly up to the sky. The balloon had been put there to show it was her tenth birthday and she was having a party. Her guests recognised the house from it. It was before Daddy went to England, and before Mark started school, so that Mammy was at home more. Granny in the Glens was still alive. As soon as school was closed they were going to her house near the bright blue sea for their summer holiday. That was a warm sunny day, a happy day, a safe day.

Next morning was Ash Wednesday. There was frost on the grass. The white pancakes lay stiff with the cold. A magpie lifted his handsome tail on a poplar tree. He saw the pancakes. He swooped down and poked at one with his strong bill. He did not like the cold, stiff stuff but there was nothing else for him. The children were still in bed. He saw smoke rising from a neighbour's chimney. Somebody had just lit the fire. He lifted the frozen pancake in his bill and flew to the chimney. He held it over the smoke till it warmed. He carried it, floppy in his bill, to his mate beside a big bundle of twigs in the poplar tree. She tore out a lump of smoked pancake. Smoked ham, smoked salmon, smoked trout, why not smoked pancake. She ate it because she was hungry.

The male magpie went back to the second pancake and brought it, too, back to the warm chimney. The smoke was gone now because only smokeless coal was allowed. He heated the pancake against the chimney pot and ate it there in the warmth. The third pancake still lay on the cold ground. He toasted it till its edges were crispy and the middle was soft. He was tempted to stay and eat it as well but he saw his mate perched beside the twigs they were building into a nest. He carried the pancake to the tree and they ate it together.

CHAPTER 2

THE SMALL BOY, MARK, got out of bed and went to the window in his pyjamas. The radiator was warm. He saw the magpies in the tree with the pancake. He laughed.

'The magpies are eating the pancakes from Granny's garden,' he said.

'Don't tell Granny,' his brother said from the pillow.

'Why not? She likes the birds to eat her stuff,' Mark said, rubbing his hand through his hair.

'She doesn't allow magpies in her garden,' Ben told him.

'Why?'

'They eat young birds. They steal eggs from other birds' nests,' Ben said, stretching himself.

'Why do they make themselves so horrible when they are such handsome birds?' Mark said, enjoying the sound of the words.

When they went down for breakfast Granny had the table set with mugs that the boys had brought from home for milk, and Hannah's china cup. Hannah did not like milk. This had worried their mother, who had bought her funny mugs first to tempt her to drink milk, and finally a china cup and saucer. She was afraid Hannah would not have good bones and teeth but Hannah was happy to eat cheese instead. She still kept her pretty china cup.

Hannah was twelve, nearer thirteen, so she went to the school for the big girls down the road from Granny's. The two boys had to go further up the road to the school near their own house, now empty. Ben took Mark by the hand

and Granny warned Mark to do what Ben said and to wait for him after school, not to go running home to his own house. Sometimes Mark was a bit dreamy. They would all be back by four o'clock.

Granny put bread out for the birds and cleared up the kitchen. She poured herself another cup of tea and sat in her armchair with her feet up on a stool in front of her. She was happy to have the children while their mother was on a course in England, but she worried that they would be unhappy away from home. Their father had worked in London for the last two years because his job in Belfast had closed down. Granny was his mother. She had two daughters as well, married in America with children of their own. Granny felt the day long sometimes with nobody to cook for. That Ash Wednesday she baked brown bread and currant scones. The kitchen was warm but it was cold outside.

At three o'clock she thought she'd go down the garden to see if there was any parsley to look pretty on the children's dinners. She knew there would not be much since there was no one to look after the garden since her husband had died. There was a path made of concrete slabs down to his greenhouse, neglected now with nothing but sad old Growbags inside. As Granny turned round at the door her heel slipped on a muddy bit. She skidded and fell on the path, knocking her head on the corner of the greenhouse. There she lay. In a heap.

The male magpie was swooping round his tree in perfect parabolas. His mate was watching him. They had been together for ten years. He did not show off to please her

8

any more. He flew to please himself and she was not impressed. She could perform an arabesque as well as he could any day.

He saw the strange navy object on the ground beside the greenhouse. He swooped down and walked around it, looking. He went clack, clack, clack. His mate came down too. They strutted around, pushing at her legs with their beaks, but Granny did not move. It was unusual.

'It's that old bag that won't let us in her garden,' the female magpie said.

'You're only an old mag yourself,' he said, making fun.

'No older than you, sweetie pie.' She flew round him. 'Why does she not like us?' she wondered.

'We eat her precious little birds,' he said.

'They eat chickens, don't they?' she said, 'and lambs, and heifers and pigs.'

'But they don't kill them. They get them in shops,' he said.

'Somebody kills them,' she said and then went on: 'How about the thrushes? They kill snails — bang the shells against the path and swallow the slimy titbits inside!'

'But snails are not pretty and thrushes are,' he explained.

'Are we not pretty!' she demanded.

'Ah — we are beautiful, a very different thing,' he said.

Then Granny's foot gave a jerk so they flew away. But they were back clack-ack-acking when Hannah came home and found the house empty.

CHAPTER 3

T HE BREAD AND SCONES were on the cooler by the table. They were still warm. She was hungry for a scone and a cup of tea with her grandmother before her brothers came in. But she went upstairs to change out of her school uniform. It was cold outside so she put on her jeans and a blouse and jumper. 'Granny must have gone into a house nearby, or out to a shop for something,' she thought. She picked up a scone but put it back again, thinking it would only be good manners to wait for Granny. The magpies were making a fearful racket at the bottom of the garden. They were in the garden, not just overflying, which Granny permitted.

Then she noticed Granny's shoes at the back door and her garden shoes which lived on the mat were gone. She opened the door and called, 'Granny, Granny, are you out there? I'm home.' Her mother always said, 'I'm home,' as soon as she came into their house. The magpies rose and circled. Hannah flapped her arms at them as she went down the path. She saw Granny lying on the ground beside the greenhouse and she stopped and said, 'Oh,' her hands clasped up on her chest. She forced herself to feel Granny's cheek. It was cold. 'Oh Granny,' she said and when Granny didn't stir she began to whisper, 'Mammy, Mammy, what will I do?' She wanted to move her grandmother, she looked so twisted and uncomfortable. But First Aid people always said you should never move such a person for fear of doing damage to the spine or head or something.

Then she pulled herself together. She ran back into the house and phoned for an ambulance. She got an old rug upstairs that they used in the summer to lie on the grass in the sun. She spread it carefully over her grandmother, trying to stop crying. She thought she'd better go back to the house to watch out of the front window for the ambulance. It seemed hours. She felt guilty leaving her grandmother alone. She wondered should she knock next door and ask for help but she didn't really know the people well. Instead, she stayed where she was, in a state.

When the ambulance stopped outside on the road, she ran out to them. 'It's my grandmother. She's unconscious. She's lying down in the garden. She's not dead, but.'

'All right, love,' one of them said. 'Are you in charge here?'

They came in through the comfortable, bread-smelling house.

'I'm only in from school,' Hannah said. 'This is how I found things.'

You're a great girl,' they told her when they saw the rug. 'And you didn't move her? What's her name?'

Hannah had to think. She couldn't remember. People didn't call her grandmother anything except Mrs Agnew or Granny or Mam or Mother.

'God, those birds!' one of the men said. 'Did you ever hear such a fuss?' The magpies were flying up and down from the poplar tree.

'It's Peggie,' Hannah remembered suddenly, 'or Margaret maybe since you don't know her well.'

They laughed and said, 'We'll try Peggie.' They spoke clearly, carefully. 'Peggie, can you hear me? You fell and

11

hurt yourself. We're just putting you on a stretcher to take you to hospital. Can you hear me, Peggie?' They eased her under her arms and she groaned and Hannah thought what a beautiful sound it was. She had been afraid her grandmother really was dead.

They carried the stretcher carefully out the narrow garden path. They asked Hannah if she was going with her grandmother. She said yes, she supposed she should, although she would not know what to do. The older man said, 'Put on a coat, love, it'll be cold later on when you're coming back,' and the other one said, 'It's cold now, Jack. Perishing!' So Hannah ran upstairs to get her jacket and remembered to put money in her pocket and the door key.

The big hospital was down the road, nearly opposite Hannah's school, but before they arrived, her grandmother was moving her head and her feet were rubbing against each other, so that the ambulance man with her was able to say, 'There you are, love — she's going to be all right,' and then in that clear voice, 'Peggie, you're in the ambulance. You're going to the hospital — the Royal. You're all right.'

Inside, Hannah told the nurse Granny's name and address. She didn't know her age because Granny kept her age a secret, even when Daddy teased her. She gave his name as next of kin, but said she hoped they wouldn't phone him in London unless Granny was very ill. She then had to sit and wait a long, long time before she was let into the cubicle where her grandmother was lying on a trolley with a blue blanket over her, dressed in a paper gown.

'A little concussion,' the nurse said. 'So we'll keep her in overnight. And her wrist is to be set — it's a Colles' fracture. But you don't have to worry. You'll be home in time for tea.'

Granny's eyes were closed and she looked really old. 'She feels the cold,' Hannah said. 'She won't be warm enough like that. Grandad used always to ask her if she was warm enough.' Granny's eyes opened and she smiled. 'He did, didn't he! This is Hannah, nurse. She's a great girl.' They put another blanket over her and she said goodnight to Hannah sleepily.

CHAPTER 4

T HE MINUTE SHE OPENED the door her two brothers attacked her. 'Where were you? Where is Granny? Why is there no dinner? We're hungry.'

Hannah began to shiver. In little bits of sentences she told them what had happened.

'Why didn't you leave a note?' Ben said. 'We thought you had been kidnapped or shot.'

'Nobody shoots grannies,' Mark said, but Ben answered 'Indeed they do, or they did. I remember reading that in the papers. At least I think I did.'

'When will our dinner be ready?' Mark asked.

'I don't know,' Hannah said. 'I'm too tired. I couldn't eat anything.'

'I'll make dinner for Mark and me,' Ben said, and he looked in the fridge and the cupboards until he found sausages and potatoes and carrots. There was liver, too, that Granny would have cooked, but when they saw how bloody it was they decided it was meant for tomorrow. Hannah just sat in Granny's armchair. Mark began to push at her and tell her that she should be laying the table but Ben looked at her pale face and told Mark to leave her alone.

'I'll make you a cup of tea afterwards,' he said. 'But if I take my eye off these sausages they'll burn.'

The sausages and carrots were ready before the potatoes were boiled but that did not worry the two boys. They ate them straight away and two potatoes each afterwards. There

14

were potatoes left because they had boiled too many. They put them aside.

'What will we say if Mammy phones?' Ben said.

'But she won't phone until Friday,' Mark said.

'She phones every night,' Hannah said. 'Only it's late when she can phone and Granny was afraid you would be begging to stay up. I heard Granny talking to her last night around ten o'clock.'

'Then we'll tell her to come home,' Mark said, smiling.

'No we won't,' the two older children said together. 'We don't want her to be worried.'

'We won't answer the phone. We'll let it ring,' Ben said.

'No we can't do that. She'd think we were all dead or something,' Hannah said.

'We'll take the phone off the hook when we're going to bed,' Ben said. 'She'll think Granny is talking to somebody else.'

'It's against the law,' said Hannah.

'Who cares!' Ben answered. They decided that if their mother rang while Hannah or Ben was up, they would not mention Granny's fall. They would say everything was lovely, but Granny had been tired with all the extra cooking and had gone to bed early with her book.

'We'll say we ate the liver,' Mark said and they all laughed and Hannah began to feel that if she made some tea she could eat a scone before the boys had them all finished.

'Who will get us out to school in the morning?' Mark asked.

'We'll get ourselves out,' Ben said, and Hannah nodded because she did not want to speak with her mouth full.

15

And they did — made breakfast and packed lunches, washed up, put their clothes in the washing machine and locked the doors. Hannah was a bit worried about shopping but she thought she would deal with that when she came home from school.

CHAPTER 5

WHEN SHE DID COME HOME Granny was sitting in her armchair in the kitchen looking very pale and tired but with a fixed polite smile because her next door neighbour, Mrs McGovern, was sitting on the edge of a hard chair.

'I just had to come in when I saw your poor grandmother arriving in a taxi with her arm in a sling,' she gushed. 'And no one to look after her.'

'Mrs McGovern has been very kindly keeping me company for nearly an hour now. She was waiting for you to come home, Hannah. So now I'm sure she has a lot to do in her own house. Hannah, if you'd see Mrs McGovern out,' Granny said.

Hannah thought this was a bit tart. She felt herself blush. She could never get rid of people like that. Neither could her mother. Maybe old age made people harder.

'If there's anything I can do now, dear,' Mrs McGovern said, 'just ask. I know Mrs Agnew keeps herself to herself, but there are times you have to forget that. I'll be glad to help.' Hannah smiled.

'Oh, I thought I'd never be left in peace,' Granny said, when Hannah came back in. 'They ordered a taxi for me in the hospital and of course I had no coat or hat and no handbag. I was disgraced. I felt so ashamed in the taxi with no money. I had no key of course but I always have one left with Mrs Lynch so I got that and went upstairs to find money for the taximan. And when I came downstairs, there

Mrs McGovern was in the hall. I couldn't get rid of her. I was so glad to see you, Hannah.'

'I'll make you a cup of tea,' Hannah said. 'And then I'd better see what I should get in the shops.'

'You are a good girl,' Granny said and closed her eyes. Her right arm was in a sling and she held it carefully across her waist. Her fingers, Hannah noticed, were swollen.

'Can you manage?' she asked, presenting the cup of tea. 'Granny, can you manage?' she repeated to make Granny open her eyes. 'You'll feel better when you've had your tea.'

'Yes of course I will,' her grandmother said, and shifted herself painfully to let her left hand do all the work. 'You'll have to help me a lot for the next week or so,' she said. 'I'm sorry about that. I wanted to give you children a warm comfortable home while your mother was away, to let you see how nice it was to have someone to welcome you every day. And now here I am — useless. But it's Lent. I'll offer it up and maybe you'll do that too.' Her cup rattled in the saucer because her left hand was unused to holding it.

Hannah felt awkward and she was wondering how soon she could get out to buy food for the dinner, and indeed what she should buy.

'I don't mind at all,' she said. 'You can show me all the things to do. I don't know much about how to bake and cook. If you teach me, I can surprise Mammy when she comes home at Easter. You don't want to send for Mammy now, do you?'

'Oh certainly not,' Granny said. 'She has to have her chance at that course. It's not as if she was my daughter.'

Hannah thought that Granny would not have made that

remark if she had been in full possession of herself.

'I'll do the messages,' Hannah said, and with Granny's advice she made out a list, was given the money and was glad to leave the house.

When she came back her two brothers were there eating bananas and bread, and her grandmother was sitting up looking more cheerful. She was telling them she had a Colles' fracture.

'Where's your colles,' Ben asked, poking at his own arm. 'I never heard of that bone.'

Granny explained, laughing a little. 'He was a doctor, I think. Imagine having a broken wrist called after you.'

Between them they managed to cook the dinner. Granny told them what to do. Ben peeled the potatoes, announcing that it was a harder job than he'd thought.

'And a slower one,' Hannah said, and wished she hadn't. She did most of the cooking. They did without dessert but there was a fruit cake in the cake tin. Granny sat up to the table but Ben cut up her meat for her. She made a joke about her second childhood.

'When Mammy rings,' Hannah asked, 'what will you say? She will think she has to come home.'

The phone rang before any of them had gone to bed and Hannah answered it while Granny was getting up out of her chair.

'We're doing great, Mammy,' Hannah said, happy to hear her mother's voice. 'Granny hurt her wrist so we're looking after everything. How is it in Bristol?'

Then Granny took up the phone. 'Yes, a stupid twist on my wrist. It's a bit sore, but nothing really. And I'm very glad to have your wonderful children here. They are as good as gold. Now I'll not keep you. Mark is jumping up and down to say hello.'

He did and said he was being very good, and then Ben grabbed the phone for his turn before Mark would let the cat out of the bag. They all heaved a sigh of relief and beamed at one another.

The next problem was how to help Granny to bed. Hannah said, 'Granny, I'll not go to bed until after you've had your bath safely. You might need help.' She did not like the thought of helping an old woman in the bath. But she need not have worried. Granny did not want that either. It was Ben who fixed up a stool beside the bath so that her plastered arm could lean on it to keep it dry. He filled her bath, put down the bath mat and left a big towel ready for her. She would have to wash with her left hand. Hannah hovered outside the bathroom door, warning her to be careful and not to slip, and offering help. When Granny came out, warm and tired, she said, 'It's only a matter of working out which arm to put first. But so far so good.'

The children went to bed and Granny went downstairs to watch television because she feared she would not be comfortable in bed. Hannah lay awake for a while in the small bedroom that used to be her father's. She was waiting until she heard Granny come up but she fell asleep and didn't wake up until the alarm clock rang.

Granny was dozing when they brought up her breakfast because she had wakened often during the night, every time she moved her arm.

'Do you know I won't chase magpies any more,' she said, while Hannah and Ben fixed her tray so that she could get at it without hurting herself.

'Why do you say that ?' Ben asked. He could hear them out in the tree as noisy and discordant as ever.

'They looked after me when I fell,' Granny said. 'They kept me company. They had a very odd conversation.'

'Is your tea all right?' Hannah asked.

'One of them wanted to bring food and drop it for me, and the other one asked if he thought he was a raven. They thought they were cousins of ravens but they weren't sure.'

'Can you butter your toast?' Hannah asked while Ben rolled his eyes at her and Mark pointed one finger to his head.

'Maybe you'd better do it for me,' Granny said. 'They were also of the opinion that we were no better than they were because we eat chickens and animals generally.'

'We have to go to school now,' Hannah said. 'Will you manage yourself or will I ask one of your neighbours to call in?'

'I'll be perfectly all right,' Granny said sharply. 'It's only my wrist that's broken, not my legs or my head.'

Hannah was not happy on the way to school. She was afraid she could not cope if Granny was going to be dotty. And for the next week Granny was very helpless. The children left her in bed in the morning and when Hannah came home in the afternoon she found her asleep in the chair. Often she did not know what day it was, or what time of the day. Sometimes she called Hannah Miriam or Anne, the names of her own daughters, Hannah's aunts in America.

Hannah was ready to do the housework and cooking,

even to seeing about food that suddenly disappeared out of the fridge or cupboards. But she had little time for homework. She got her written work done but she was supposed to think of a geography project – or coursework as it was called in this school. Not even once had her mind settled enough to find an idea.

'I wish someone was in charge,' she said out loud during geography class, with her mind a mile away.

'Indeed Hannah,' Miss Sterling said, while the class tittered. 'I had prided myself that I was in charge.'

Hannah's face went redder than her wine-coloured uniform. Miss Sterling was straight and narrow. Her hair was set in stiff ridges, beige to match the beige suits she wore, year in, year out.

'And now that we have your attention, what about your project? We all depend on you to be intelligent.'

Hannah was not sure if she was being sarcastic.

'I haven't quite begun,' she stammered.

'Not quite? And why have you not quite begun, may I ask?'

Hannah was now quite sure she was being sarcastic.

'I'm staying in my grandmother's house,' she said lamely.

'But I know your grandmother,' Miss Sterling said. 'I taught your aunts. Your grandmother is not illiterate. She is an excellent woman. She would not approve of your laziness. Let me have no more of these excuses. You should be ashamed of yourself.'

Hannah sat down, mute. Girls never explained things to Miss Sterling – that was the kind of teacher she was.

'Why did you not tell her your Granny was in hospital?'

one of the girls said after class because everyone on the road knew about her Granny on a stretcher going off in the ambulance.

'Because she's not,' Hannah snapped.

'Oh excuse me!' the girl said and her friends laughed with her. Hannah trudged back to her grandmother's house, telling herself that everyone hated her.

The male magpie was flying over Agnews' garden with a twig in his beak. He glanced down and he dropped it. He didn't fly down to pick it up.

'Plenty more where it came from,' he said to Mags when he landed on the poplar tree, so gracefully that the branch didn't sway.

'You're afraid of the old woman,' his mate jeered.

'She's not here any more,' he said, taking a turn about the tree. 'Not a sign of her. Look for yourself. No bread out for days for the birds she likes. She's gone.'

Mags flew over Agnews' old apple tree.

'Oh poor hop-a-lilty! left all alone to die – starving. She's been hopping there, getting bread all winter,' she said, watching a lame blackbird.

'She can get worms, can't she,' her mate said. 'She shouldn't depend on the old woman.'

'Look, look, look.' Mags clacked. 'You're wrong. You know nothing. There's the old bat herself coming out the back door.' She swept back to her own tree.

'She's odd looking,' her mate said. 'She's throwing out the crumbs all wrong, all jerky. She's only got one arm now – do you see!'

'Poor old bat,' Mags said. 'Will she end up like hop-

23

a-lilty with only a bent arm hanging useless instead of a bent leg?'

'No, no, the arm's gone,' he said. 'She must have knocked it off when we found her on the ground.'

He flew over to the greenhouse and walked around on the muddy ground and Mrs Agnew didn't chase him at all.

'Hello magpie,' she called and the magpie nearly died of shock, while his mate nearly killed herself laughing. A magpie laugh is not a pretty sound.

CHAPTER 6

'OH DEAR,' GRANNY SAID when Hannah came in. 'Not the best day you ever had, I can see.'

Hannah was startled into a smile. 'Never mind,' Granny went on. 'Tomorrow's Friday and we'll get a lot of things settled over the weekend. I was out at the shops today and I feel much better.'

She didn't look much better. Her hair was not quite right because she had to comb it with her left hand. 'Mrs Lynch brought in buns for your tea. Isn't it very kind of her.'

Hannah agreed but she remembered her mother saying to her father, 'It would be much easier for your mother if she'd let people be kind to her. But oh no, she needs nobody.' Hannah belonged to that large group of girls who overhear everything they are not expected to hear.

'I'm sure all your neighbours would be very glad to help if they knew what you would like,' Hannah said, as she went back with the tea to Granny. 'The buns look lovely,' she said, biting into one with her cup of tea. But Granny had dropped asleep with her tea beside her. Hannah sighed. When her brothers came in they ate three buns each and smacked their lips in a way that Hannah told them was quite disgusting. They laughed at her and so did Granny. She sulked while she scrubbed the potatoes and washed the celery. 'I'm good enough for this kind of job. They don't like me, any of them, but they'll let me clean vegetables for them. I wish Mammy was home,' she said in her mind. She didn't cry because she was too cross. She wouldn't let them see that she minded. But behind her back Granny was making signs to her brothers that they were to be nice to her.

She cut the celery in inch lengths into a saucepan, put in a little salt and pepper and then took a milk bottle from the fridge to cover the bottom of the pot.

'What are you doing?' Granny asked sharply, surprised.

'I'm putting on the celery,' Hannah answered, equally surprised.

'I never saw it cooked that way,' Granny said.

'That's the way Mammy does it,' Hannah said. 'All the good stays in it. She says celery stops people getting rheumatism. At least Grandad in Cushendall told her that was why he had neither pain nor ache. When the celery is almost tender I will put in a little cornflour to thicken the sauce. Sometimes, then, Mammy puts in parsley.'

'Maybe I should go down the garden to see is there any!' Granny said, smiling.

'And break the other arm,' Hannah said, and they both laughed.

'It's my homework,' Hannah explained. 'I haven't been doing it properly and Miss Sterling was at me about my geography coursework.

'Miss Sterling,' Granny exclaimed. 'Is that old knitting needle still teaching? Mind you, Miriam and Anne used to say she was a good teacher. But she has a sharp tongue.'

'She says you are an excellent woman,' Hannah said.

'Well then, I'll have to live up to that. We'll think of something. Have you geography tomorrow or will it do over the weekend?'

Hannah said Monday would be fine and since Grandfather, who was dead, had once taught geography in a boys' school, Hannah was hopeful that the void in her brain would be filled. She was cheerful enough talking to Mammy on the phone, which was just as well because Mammy prided herself on knowing how her children felt.

On Friday afternoon when Hannah said goodbye to the two girls who walked as far as Granny's gate with her, Mrs McGovern came to the door and beckoned her.

'Hannah,' she said. 'Your name is Hannah, isn't it? How is Mrs Agnew? I don't want to bother her but I would like to be helpful. Your mother used to drive her to the shops on Saturday, and of course your mother's away – isn't she? I could drive her but if I offer she'll say no. She is a very proud woman.'

Hannah didn't say anything but she smiled at Mrs McGovern to show she sympathised

'Could you persuade her?' Mrs McGovern said, 'and of course you would need to come too, to help her with her shopping. What do you think?'

'I'll say yes,' Hannah said, nodding vigorously. 'I am very grateful to you. Maybe if she is too tired in the morning, my brothers and I could take her list and your lift. She is still very shaken.'

Mrs McGovern laughed a bit. 'You're a good girl. I just want to be a good neighbour.'

'That awful woman,' Granny said when she was told. So Hannah didn't know what was to be done in the morning.

However, before she could get into a state, her grandmother said, 'I want you to look in the bottom of the big bookcase in the dining room. I have a great idea for your project.'

'What am I to look for?' Hannah asked, opening the carved mahogany door.

'A wad of graph books – exercise books,' Granny said. 'They could well be behind other books. I thought I'd have them out for you but it was beyond me even without my Colles' fracture.'

'Would you like your cup of tea first?' Hannah asked. 'How are you today?'

'I'm getting better,' Granny said. 'I'm not so tired and my fingers are not so swollen. I'm still sore, but only my arm, not all over me.' She smiled the way she used to smile, not pathetically. Hannah thought it was maybe a good idea to say, 'Will we go with Mrs McGovern to-morrow? We have to get the messages and she might be insulted if just Ben and I went. She wants to be friendly.'

Granny said, 'Huh, she wants to tell everyone how good she was.' Then she paused. 'Maybe not, God forgive me. I'm a nasty old woman. Yes, I'll go with you. We'll make a list. But find those graph books first.'

They were at the side but Hannah missed them at first because she was distracted by all the old books with dark blue, green or wine covers. The big Bible was there with all the frightening pictures they used to goggle at when they came to visit before their grandfather died. Hannah put it to one side. The *Flight of the Eagle* she read out. *Ulrich the Ready*, *Traits and Stories of the Irish Peasantry*. She opened that one but the print was tiny and the pages blotched. By that time Ben was there too with *Red Cloud* and *Kidnapped* and Mark was shouting that he wanted some with pictures. Granny took him away to find some Doctor Seuss books that their daddy used to have. 'Are you my Mother?' she and Mark began to read – mostly Granny because Mark was not a great reader yet. But he remembered the words easily enough.

At last the bundle of graph books fell out at Hannah's knees because the books supporting them had been moved. Hannah opened one. Each page of little squares had a red line and under it a blue line jerking from the left side to near the right edge. There were figures along the bottom of the page and up the left side. Hannah was puzzled – even when she saw the name of the month at the top of each page. The last one was January 1992.

Granny looked at it sadly. 'That's the last month your grandfather took the temperatures. I should have kept on taking them after he died. I would have if I'd thought you could use them. But I didn't think.' She sat with the open page on her knee.

'I don't understand what it's about,' Hannah said.

'Oh I do.' Ben looked at it. 'Grandfather explained it all to me when I was younger.'

'Well go on then. What is it?' Hannah said impatiently.

Ben took a deep breath and began. 'Well, you know the thermometer nailed to a post at the end of the garden? Grandfather used to go down to it every morning with a magnet. The thermometer has two tubes. One showed the highest temperature it had been since he fixed it with the magnet. The other showed the lowest temperature. Grandfather then pulled the indicators back to the temperature at that moment. He came back in and said to Granny, "Twelve and five" or "Twenty and twelve" or whatever it was. I heard him. And he wrote it into the book in those squares. The red line shows the highest and the blue line the lowest for each day. It's called maximum and minimum. Isn't that right, Granny?'

'Spoken like a professor,' Granny said, smiling in admiration.

'I see,' Hannah said, studying one of the pages. When she looked at the figures she could understand. The figures at the bottom were the dates of the month and the ones at the side were the temperatures in Centigrade degrees. 'But what can I do with these?' she wondered.

Ben was sorting them out. 'The earliest is January 1972.' He was excited at a record going back so far.

'They used to go further back than that,' Granny said. 'But the earlier ones were on big sheets of paper that we kept up on the kitchen door so that your Daddy and Miriam and Anne could see them clearly each day. They had the job of filling in the lines then, so sometimes they were a bit messy. I'm afraid I put them in the bin afterwards. We did it so that they would really understand temperatures. Your Daddy would have done the same for you only he had to go away.'

'But 1972 is ages back. Daddy was seventeen then,' Ben said.

Hannah was still torturing herself about what use she could make of them to protect herself from Miss Sterling's stinging words.

'Global warming,' Ben said. 'We could see is there any sign. We've got twenty years. We'll take a date.'

'Hannah's birthday,' Granny suggested. 'Thirtieth June. Isn't that right?'

Ben was immediately turning over pages, flying from book to book to compare. '23 and 14. 19 and 13. 17 and 12. 21 and 13. 19 and 15. 20 and 12.' He was shouting.

'All right, all right,' Hannah said. 'I'll have to think what to do. I'll have to put it all in order. I'll get a new graph book tomorrow when we're out. Can I? And I'll make a graph of my birthday all down the years. And Christmas maybe. And Ben's birthday in March and one in the autumn.'

Granny was pointing at Mark and mouthing, 'Don't leave him out.'

So Hannah smiled and said they'd put in 8 September too. Mark didn't know what they were talking about but he beamed at the mention of his birthday.

'You have an orderly mind, Hannah,' Granny said. 'You will do well.'

'The thermometer is still there, isn't it Granny?' Ben asked.

'Indeed it is,' said Granny. 'Well covered with bird's dirt I can imagine. I rarely look at it.'

'Can I start a graph book of my own?' Ben asked. 'From tomorrow.'

'Why not?' said Granny. 'It's usual to begin at the start of the month. When's the first of April?'

'All Fools' Day,' said Mark, not really listening.

'But last Monday was the first of March,' Ben said.

'Was it really?' Granny said sadly. 'I thought it was much later in the month. These last two weeks have been endless. I've been so confused.' She sighed. 'First I'd better take a J-cloth down the garden and clean up the thermometer.'

'I'll go,' Ben said and Mark said, 'I'll go too,' because

31

they were embarrassed to see their Granny sad.

In the evening sunlight the two boys walked down the garden. Their shadows, one long, one shorter, fell on the ragged winter grass. The bigger boy carried a bowl of water which made him move more carefully to avoid spilling water on his legs.

The male magpie flew over, straight as a dart, to see what was happening. His mate sat on the nest.

'What are they doing?' she asked.

'Your guess is as good as mine,' he said. 'I thought they were washing the old apple tree but it's not that.'

'Even wee boys wouldn't be as daft as that,' she said.

'Have a look,' he urged.

'I can't leave the nest,' she complained.

'Only for a minute. That won't do any harm.' He took a turn about the tall tree.

'This nest is such a mess,' she clacked. 'If I don't stay sitting here holding it together, it will fall apart.'

'In ten years of making our nests not one has ever fallen apart,' he said.

'Well they always looked as if they would. They're no soft seat.'

She was cranky.

'Come on, Mags. Have a look. They're nice boys. They're brothers, I think. They both have that smooth brown hair.'

'Half the boys in Belfast have brown hair,' she said.

But while he took her place for a minute she went and perched, her plump white breast bright against the dark green of the cypress tree in the next garden. She watched Ben squeeze the blue cloth out of the suds and dab at the

32

thermometer on the brown post under the Bramley tree. She flapped round a few times to exercise her wings and puff out her chest.

'You're a right old fool, sweetie-pie,' she said complacently as she settled back in her nest. It was nice to know more than her mate.

'Well what are they doing? Are they looking for old windfall apples?' he asked.

'Not at all. The blackbirds have eaten them all,' she said. 'Do you remember the old man used to come down the garden every morning? He scattered bread for the birds that can't fend for themselves. He emptied the teapot into the rosebed and then he came down to that post with the white thing on it. He bent down looking at it, and then he touched it with a lump of red-painted metal.'

'I never knew what he was doing,' he said.

'I never knew either. They don't know about us. We don't know about them,' she said.

'It used to be nailed to the tree, that thing,' he remembered.

'So it was. That didn't do the tree any good. All one side of the tree did poorly, leaves, apples, the whole thing. At last they had the wit to shift it.'

Tomorrow morning when it's light we'll take a look to see what the thing is for,' he suggested.

'You can,' she said. 'We'll be as wise as ever but you will tell me you have the whole thing worked out.'

She cackled and he flapped at her in fun. They swooped around a few times in turn and then settled as darkness settled, leaving only a fading red behind Divis and Black Mountain.

CHAPTER 7

'THE LIST. THE SHOPPING LIST!' Granny said, as soon as the children brought up her breakfast. She sounded firm and wide awake so Hannah's face lost its worried frown. She ran down for a pad and biro.

'Can we get our breakfast first?' Mark asked.

'No,' Granny said. 'We'll make out our list. Then we'll have our breakfast and we'll remember all the things we've forgotten.'

'Granny, you can eat your breakfast while the tea's hot,' Hannah said. 'You can't write anyway so I'll do it.'

Ben poured her tea and put butter and marmalade on her toast. She had made the marmalade in January.

'Now,' she said. 'Let's get our minds on the job.'

'Bread, butter, tea, sugar,' Mark said because he'd heard his Daddy say that, when his mother wondered what was wanted from the shops.

'Red and blue biros and two graph books,' Ben said and Hannah wrote that down. She had to run up and downstairs checking the fridge for butter and eggs, the cupboards for flours, sugar and cereals of each kind, the garage for potatoes and vegetables, the dining room for apples, oranges, lemons and bananas. She was amazed at the organisation required. She had never noticed her mother in charge of all that but the supplies were always there.

'It's lovely buying food in quantity again,' Granny said. 'There's no good in buying stuff just for myself. I'm glad

34

you're here, children. I really am. What would I do without you!'

'Indeed, Granny, what would you do without me!' Mark said, climbing up on her bed and rocking the tray perilously.

At eleven o'clock, Mrs McGovern rang the doorbell and Granny thanked her graciously. They all trooped to the car.

'Oh! are they all coming?' Mrs McGovern said doubtfully, so that Hannah began to understand Granny's dislike of her. However she inquired after Granny's arm and general health, and how she was managing in the house. The three children sat in silence in the back seat, Hannah with the list in her hand. Granny was being very, very grateful to Mrs McGovern when they climbed out of the car at the block of shops and settled a time to be driven back. Granny asked Mrs McGovern would she have a cup of coffee perhaps at the café just round the corner but Mrs McGovern said oh no she had far too much work to do at home. Hannah looked warningly at her two brothers in case they would say something nasty. They always imagined grown-ups didn't hear them when they said things like 'Silly cow' or 'Old eejit'. Granny pursed her lips and assured her they wouldn't keep her too long at the shops.

Inside, Granny met women she knew, one after the other. Some were old like herself, some were Mammy's age. Most knew about her accident. They sympathised with her and asked how they could help. The children waited beside her. Hannah and Ben would have filled the trolley but they wanted the word from Granny. At last Granny said, 'Goodness, Mrs McGovern is being very kindly and giving us a lift, and she's in a hurry.' The other woman laughed and said, 'Don't hurry. I'll leave you home. Tell Mrs McGovern you've met an old friend and I'll see you in the café. But I'm in no rush at all. I'm happy to sit there till lunchtime.'

'How will we find Mrs McGovern?' Granny murmured and Mark shouted, 'I'll find her. I'll tell her we don't need her.'

'Oh Mark, Mark, keep quiet,' Granny said. 'Hannah, can I trust you to put it nicely? We've just met an old friend who insists on looking after us. We're very grateful to her for bringing us here. We could not have managed without her.'

'Of course we could, old witch,' Ben said and Granny told him, 'We couldn't you know. But come on, we've a job to do,' and round the shelves they went. They were nearly finished when Hannah joined them, panting.

'What did she say?' Granny asked.

'That she was glad to be of help, and she would do anything any time,' Hannah answered, thinking she might be grateful for help.

They relaxed in the warmth of the coffee shop. Other customers brought chairs round for them and the girl behind the counter brought over the trays of coffee and orange juice and biscuits and buns. Granny laughed and talked to her friend, describing her difficulties dressing herself. She told about the children buttering her bread and cutting her meat as if they'd all had a great time. A bit of pink even appeared in her cheeks.

But when they went out with their bags to the woman's

car she said to Hannah, 'Help me to put these in the boot.'

'I will,' Ben said.

'No, no, just Hannah.' Then when Hannah was beside her: 'You'll have to tell your mother to come home, Mrs Agnew is very failed.'

'She is much better now,' Hannah said, although her heart had begun to thump.

'It would be dreadful, Hannah, if anything were to happen – not that I want to frighten you – but your mother's place is with her mother now.'

'She's not her mother,' Hannah said abruptly.

'Oh?' the woman said, her eyebrows raised.

'Granny is my Daddy's mother and my mother is on a very important course,' Hannah went on, thinking that this woman would consider her a rude young madam.

'Ah well,' the woman said with a stiff laugh, 'It's still the woman's job to look after the old people, dear.'

'I'll write to my Daddy,' Hannah said.

'And ring the doctor,' the woman said. 'Mrs Agnew tells me Dr McHenry hasn't seen her at all. That's not right, you know.'

She banged down the boot and when they were in the car she said, 'There we are now, all packed and happy.'

Hannah was not happy, not happy at all. The day was spoilt for her. The woman insisted on giving a pound each to Hannah and Ben and fifty pence to Mark. Hannah didn't like taking money but Granny didn't support her.

'Isn't Mrs Lynch a very nice woman,' Granny said, as Ben helped her off with her coat the way she had shown him, and Mark waited to take her hat upstairs. Hannah was busy putting away the food.

'I'd rather have Mrs McGovern,' she muttered, so that Ben laughed, not knowing what she was talking about. Hannah wondered if she should tell him. She decided not to. She remembered hearing her mother's mother say to her mother, 'Keep it to yourself, love. A trouble shared is a trouble doubled.' She never knew what they were discussing but the words stayed in her mind. She had been very fond of Granny in the Glens.

How could she ring the doctor without Granny knowing, when the telephone was in the hall. Granny showed no sign of going asleep. After lunch, Granny did doze and Hannah looked up the phone book and rang Dr McHenry. But it was Saturday afternoon and the phone just rang and rang.

'Who are you ringing up?' Mark asked and Hannah said 'Nobody,' quite truthfully. Ben was busy drawing lines in his graph book and writing figures up one side and along the bottom.

'You're supposed to be at your temperatures,' he told her. 'I'll lend you my ruler.'

So they sat together at the kitchen table and ruled their pages and drew in the numbers and hunted back all through their grandfather's sheets of paper. By bedtime they were very pleased with themselves. Ben's business was much shorter so he was happy to keep track of the temperatures down the twenty years. He was excited at the similarities on the same dates.

'Oh I must keep this up,' he said over and over again. 'This is very interesting. What will I do for a thermometer? When we go home at Easter I can't run round here every morning.'

Hannah told him to shush for fear Granny would think he was begging for hers but Granny said, 'You're welcome to this one, Ben, but I'm sure your Daddy will buy you one when he knows you're so keen. The best way of showing that is to keep your graph filled up very neatly until you do go home.'

'I have a birthday coming up. I'll be eleven on 21 March,' Ben said.

'Oh we'll not forget that,' Granny assured him. 'But I'm afraid we'll not be able to manage a party.'

'I'm too old for a party,' Ben laughed. 'Only people Mark's age have parties.'

'When can I have a party?' Mark asked but they all laughed and Ben took him off to bath and bed.

CHAPTER 8

ON MONDAY HANNAH COULD HARDLY WAIT for geography class. She had all her homework carefully done. Although she was busy with housework Granny insisted that she be left in peace on Sunday afternoon to prepare all her work. Granny and the two boys took the Sunday papers and their books into the sitting room where the television was, and Hannah spread out her books in the kitchen. To begin with, she worried about ringing the doctor or writing to her father and then she thought she'd get on with her own work.

'Hannah this is amazing,' Miss Sterling said. 'I knew we could depend on you for something intelligent.' She was studying the graph. 'Did you make up those temperatures?'

'Oh no,' said Hannah, shocked.

'You are a real scientist,' Miss Sterling nodded. 'Where did you find all this information?'

'In my grandfather's records,' Hannah said. She had planned this. She thought it sounded rather well.

'Aren't you lucky to have such a grandfather,' Miss Sterling said.

'He's dead,' Hannah said. 'My grandmother kept his records. I made up a graph of the temperatures on those dates. He had pages and pages – one for every month.' She didn't want Miss Sterling to think she had just copied something already there.

'Well now,' Miss Sterling said, 'your next job is to write a page or two drawing conclusions. We'll not spoil the story by pointing out now what you should say.'

Some of the girls wanted to know how it was possible to find out temperatures since the only thermometer they knew was for sick people. Miss Sterling was a strict disciplinarian so she put a stop to that. She told them she'd prepare a lesson on it for Thursday. Then they would know the following Monday what Hannah was talking about. Hannah was content.

On her way home she went into a phone box with two of her friends to ring Dr McHenry. It was a bit of a crush and the other two girls were giggling. When the doctor's receptionist answered the telephone Hannah asked if the doctor would please call on Mrs Agnew who had broken her arm.

'When did this happen? Can she come into the surgery?' the woman asked.

'Over a week ago – longer than that,' Hannah stumbled.

'Did she have it set in hospital? Did she go straight to the hospital?' she was asked.

'Yes, that's right,' Hannah agreed.

'Well then the hospital is looking after her. It's nothing to do with us.' And the phone was put down.

'Oh thank you,' Hannah said into the receiver and they all burst out laughing. But when she was at Granny's door she asked herself, 'What am I supposed to do now?'

She heard voices in the sitting room. 'This is Maeve, dear,' Granny said. 'She is torturing me. She is a physio-therapist and she is helping me to get my arm ready to work again. I met her at the church yesterday and she very kindly offered to show me what exercises I should do.'

Maeve smiled and then went back to the broken arm, telling Granny to drop her hand forward from her wrist over the end of the chair arm. She wouldn't stay for tea because she had another appointment. She told Granny to keep up the exercises.

'Oh Hannah, you don't know the half of it,' Granny laughed. 'I'm ready for this tea. Those exercises really hurt me but I'm sure they'll do me good. I've to have a hammer in for the next session and an umbrella. When I was young they always said if it didn't hurt you it did no good. But I thought that was gone.'

The two boys were home from school and Hannah was recounting the success of grandfather's 'records' when the doorbell rang twice, peremptorily. Hannah opened the door and a tall man carrying a small case stepped in. 'Who are you?' Hannah demanded, blocking the way.

'Quite the guard-dog! I've come to see Mrs Agnew. I'm Dr McHenry.'

'Oh come in,' Hannah said, blushing. She thought he might have said who he was before stepping in. 'Your secretary said you wouldn't come.'

'That's my dragon,' he said. 'Mrs Agnew has a guard-dog. I have a dragon.'

Hannah didn't think he was very funny and later in the evening she and Ben enjoyed themselves imitating him. But he was charming to Granny, who was flustered because she had not expected him. The children left the room while he was there but Hannah waited to see him out. He pinched her cheek, which annoyed her, but he told her Granny was fine 'heart, lungs, liver and all' except for her broken arm, of course, and the hospital would look after that.

That night Hannah looked for an envelope and paper. Pretending she was still at her homework, she wrote to her father, telling him what had happened and that his mother was fine. She warned him not to tell Mammy or she'd want to fly home to look after her family. She also mentioned Ben's birthday in case he forgot. She knew her mother would remember. It was such a relief to have told somebody in charge that she forgot to buy a stamp and post it until nearly the end of the week. But it didn't matter because Granny obviously grew more capable every day.

She was due in the hospital for a check-up and X-ray to see that her wrist was setting in the right place.

'This sling is filthy,' she said. 'I can't go to the hospital with it. We've washed it and ironed it over and over but it doesn't please me.'

'It's grotty,' Hannah agreed.

'We'll go into town, you and I, to buy some calico — enough to make two,' Granny said. 'Will Ben and Mark be all right in the house?

'Are you sure you're able?' Hannah asked.

'Of course I am. I love town. We'll take a taxi in and out.' Granny was quite like her old self.

'Maybe I should ask Mrs McGovern, next door, to keep an eye on the house while Ben and Mark are on their own,' Hannah said.

'Oh do you think so?' Granny said doubtfully. 'Ben is very sensible.'

'Yes he is,' Hannah agreed, 'but he's not very old.'

So that was arranged with smiles from Mrs McGovern and with scowls from Ben. Granny and Hannah went off in a taxi. They bought the cloth and looked in a few shop windows and had coffee in Bewley's.

'It's lovely to have a Bewley's in Belfast now,' Hannah said, enjoying the coffee smell. Mammy would have bought something to bring home to the boys, but Granny didn't think of it and Hannah did not like to make the suggestion.

The next day Granny was back from the hospital when Hannah came in from school.

'Guess what?' Granny said.

'How is your arm?' Hannah wanted to know, because people had been telling her how some arms had to be broken again if they were not setting properly.

'Oh it's doing well,' Granny said. 'But do you know what I was told?'

'No. What?'

'I was told: "Get rid of that sling. It only hampers you. Throw it away." ' Granny laughed and so did Hannah.

'After us buying the calico and cutting it out!' Hannah said.

'I enjoyed our trip to town,' Granny said.

'So did I,' Hannah nodded.

'Mags, she's found her arm. It's stuck on with white stuff,' the male magpie said, flying back to the tree.

'What are you raving about?' his mate asked.

'I tell you,' he answered. 'I can see her two hands. She's not using her right one, but it's there.'

'I suppose she heard that a bird cannot fly on one wing – even an old bird,' she said, taking her turn off the nest.

The sun was shining and some daisies had come up in the grass. The daffodils that had been bedraggled in the rain of the previous day now basked in the spring warmth. They came up every year from the bulbs sown long ago. Mrs Agnew walked down the path.

'I will have to do something about this garden. I can't let it go like last summer. What would the neighbours say! But I can't do anything until this arm is fixed. Sure I can't, magpie?' She called the last bit to the magpie alighting for a moment on the Bramley tree. She was a bit stiff after sitting on her nest. She cocked her head, watching Mrs Agnew, waiting for her to stamp her foot and clap her hands to frighten her out of the garden.

'Ha!' she clacked. 'I'm getting as stupid as himself. She can't use her two hands to clap. That's why she's not chasing me.' That's what she told her mate when she went back to the poplar tree. But she knew it wasn't the whole story. 'She talks to herself. She's lonely.'

'Her mate's gone,' the male said, preening himself. 'Aren't you lucky, Mags!'

A cool breeze shook the tree. 'It's not summer yet,' they said together.

CHAPTER 9

T HINGS SETTLED INTO a kind of a routine with Granny able to do more cooking. Hannah had time to do her homework and reap more praise at school but she had no time for her friends, except just on the road home from school. Mrs McGovern took them for their main shopping trip on Saturday although Granny suggested that a taxi would have them under no obligation. Hannah pretended Granny was not serious and arranged things with Mrs McGovern.

'What do you think has happened?' her Granny greeted Hannah one evening when she came home. She was looking very pleased. 'Oliver rang me from London, your Daddy. It must have cost him a fortune to ring me in the middle of the day. Indeed he doesn't often ring me at all. But he says he's coming over next weekend. What do you think of that!' She beamed her delight. Hannah thought if her daddy could see the effect of his phone call, he'd ring every week. 'We'll have to clean the house from top to bottom.'

'Oh Granny,' Hannah remonstrated. 'Daddy would never notice if the house was dusty or not.'

'With these brighter days all the dust is shown up,' Granny insisted. 'We'll get it shining. We'll not bother with a cup of tea. We're getting too fat.'

Hannah laughed and produced duster and polish. Ben said he would hoover, which he did noisily and violently with Mark making engine noises after him. Hannah thought

Granny might disapprove but Granny was in such a good mood she laughed at them. 'Great,' Granny said. 'I suppose we've to make dinner now. We'll do the windows to-morrow.'

During dinner, Hannah was happy. Granny had organ-ised the cleaning, she had energy and she was able to manage her knife and fork again. Then Granny said suddenly, 'Oh, Hannah, you're sleeping in Oliver's room. Where will you go? Will you sleep on the couch in the sitting room?'

Hannah's heart sank. Such a time for Granny to get mixed up. Mark began to laugh.

'Daddy has a house. He has a whole empty house. He has four beds to sleep in. He can take turns in each bed.'

Granny nodded her head. 'Of course that would be easier, I suppose. I just wanted him to stay in his old room. I thought his house would be cold.' She looked sad.

'Mammy left the heat so that it turns on for part of each day,' Ben said. 'We could go down and see if it's all right.'

'No,' Hannah said. 'Mammy said we were not to be going back. She said you'd be bringing all kinds of stuff up to Granny's saying you needed it when you didn't at all. She said we'd never be able to keep track of you.'

'Mammy would never say such a thing,' Ben said and Mark agreed.

'She never said that, you're making it up.'

Hannah felt her cheeks go red, because it was she and not Mammy who had said that. Mammy had said they were not to go tripping up and down to their own house. That was all.

There were unhappy heads round the table until Granny cheered up and said, 'We'll make a Simnel cake for next Sunday. Ben, are you good at beating up butter and sugar?'

'I don't know,' Ben said, puzzled. 'I never have.'

'Goodness,' Granny said. 'Your Daddy was great at it. It was no trouble for me to make a cake if your Daddy was around. Does your Mammy do it all by herself?'

'She has a food processor,' Hannah said and Granny laughed.

'Of course, of course she has, and I have a wooden spoon and an egg beater. We'll bake it tomorrow when you come home from school. The windows can wait.'

'What is Simnel cake?' Mark asked. 'Will I like it?'

'It's really an Easter cake,' Granny said. 'At least I think it is. But in the days when big girls were hired out to work in richer people's farms or houses they used to be allowed home to visit on the middle Sunday in Lent and they brought home a cake, or so it says in books. I imagine it's an English custom but anyway that's next Sunday, Mother's Day or Mothering Sunday. That's why Oliver is coming to see me.'

'Maybe we should send Mammy a card,' Hannah said.

'She always said we were not to be spending Daddy's money on silly things for Mother's Day,' Ben said, still cross. He didn't know was he cross with Hannah or with his mother.

'I know she did say that,' Hannah agreed, 'but she's away now and the other mothers will get cards. She might like a letter or something.'

'I'll draw one,' Mark said and ran off to get paper and crayons.

'We'll each get a card on our way home from school,' Ben said to Hannah.

'One envelope will do to save stamps,' Hannah said.

In bed that night she wondered, just before she dropped to sleep, if it was always such hard work keeping people happy.

CHAPTER 10

NEXT DAY IN THE CARD SHOP she was trying to find something that her mother would not find too sweet and sugary. She was not a sentimental woman. Hannah could imagine her discarding all those hearts and roses. She was tempted to leave the shop empty-handed but how would she explain that to Ben.

'Hello Hannah,' she heard, and a girl from her class at school was beside her. She helped Hannah in their hunt.

'My Daddy is coming home from England at the weekend to visit Granny because of Mother's Day,' Hannah said. 'We're staying at Granny's house because Mammy is away on a course.'

The other girl said, 'My Daddy is bringing us all out to lunch in a hotel on Sunday so that my Mum won't have to work.'

'Oh isn't that a lovely idea,' Hannah said. She had never been to a hotel for lunch.

On her way up the road she remembered all the dining rooms she had seen on television with waiters in black suits and tables with white damask cloths and big napkins. If her Daddy was in charge he would know just how to cope with the menus. He'd order wine for himself and Granny. Maybe he'd even put a spoonful into Ben's glass and hers as he did sometimes when he was home. Mark sipped wine once and said he would never touch it again in his whole life. Hannah didn't really like the taste either but she loved the red colour in the glass and she quite enjoyed the smell.

'Granny,' she said, the minute she was in the door, 'will we go to a restaurant for lunch on Sunday. Daddy could bring us.'

'Oh not at all,' Granny said comfortably. Your Daddy is tired eating out in England. He'll enjoy home cooking here. We'll manage a lovely meal. Don't worry for one second about that.' And that was the end of that. Hannah's pink balloon disappeared in the bushes.

'Now for the Simnel cake,' Granny said, when Ben and Mark were each happy with a slice of fresh bread and butter. 'I've a block of margarine out of the fridge all day. It's quite soft enough to beat. When the recipe says butter I use margarine. Butter is very good for you, I will always believe, but it's too dear for me to use baking. Here, Ben, is your bowl with eight ounces of margarine and eight ounces of brown sugar. Mark, take this dish over to the fridge and lift out four eggs, carefully, mind.'

'Have I no job?' Hannah asked, wondering could she go and do some homework but not wanting to miss the mixing.

'You, Hannah,' said Granny, 'have to weigh out the fruit. My recipe says two pounds of fruit so you will decide what amount you want to put in of currants, raisins, sultanas, peel, cherries, apricots. Just so long as it mounts up to two pounds.'

The old black iron and brass scales were out on the table with the stack of weights beside it.

'But have we got currants and raisins?' Hannah asked. 'We didn't buy them lately.'

'Every self-respecting house has a store of currants,

raisins, sultanas and peel,' Granny said, smiling. 'But I went out this morning and bought cherries and the ground almonds for the icing. Ground almonds are gone very dear, I must say.'

So Hannah weighed out the fruit and snipped the apricots with the scissors. She began to cut the cherries with Granny's sharp little pointed knife. 'Some people would wash these,' she said.

'Some people have more time than sense,' Granny answered. 'They're clean from the packets and they are going to be baked. Not a germ will survive.' Granny was very self-assured in control of her squad.

In a short time Ben had his mixture looking like whipped coffee-cream, ready for the eggs. He lifted one dubiously when Granny told him to.

'Crack it,' she said. 'Crack it on the rim of the bowl.'

'Take your courage in your hand,' Hannah said, smiling. There was no difficulty in her job.

'Swop,' Ben said. 'I'll cut up those cherries. They're too sticky on your dainty fingers.'

Hannah laughed and they changed over. Hannah had cracked eggs at home many a time. So one after the other she broke them and beat them into the creamed fat and sugar. Mark weighed out eight ounces of flour, spilling quite a bit on the table, and two ounces of nuts. Hannah sifted the flour, gently folding it in.

'You never use baking powder in a rich fruit cake,' Granny said, crashing cake tins about, trying to reach the right size with her left hand. 'There's the tin still to line,' she said.

'Oh I can do that and so can Ben,' Hannah said. 'Mammy

showed us how. We are experts.' She wanted to make sure Granny knew Mammy could cook too. Ben put the tin down on the greaseproof paper and drew round it with a pencil. He cut out that circle for the bottom and then strips for the side with a fold an inch deep which he snipped so that the paper lay flat under the circle and the rest stood straight up, a little taller than the sides.

'Aren't you clever children!' Granny said.

Hannah added the fruit and suggested a little sherry or brandy. When it was spooned into the tin and smoothed over, Ben licked the wooden spoon and Mark put his fingers in round the bowl to skim out what was there. Hannah did think they were very messy but she used a teaspoon to try a little, just to see if it tasted as well as it smelled.

'We'll leave it in a cool place covered up, until tomorrow,' Granny said. 'I'll put it in the oven when I get up and when you open the door in the afternoon a lovely perfume of hot cake will waft down the hall to you.'

'Granny is getting poetic,' Ben said and Granny laughed. 'Baking does that to me.'

'When will we do the almond icing?' Hannah asked as she cleaned up. She still worried about her homework. Her geography was fine, but she had maths to do and French and English and it would pile up if she didn't do it each evening.

'The icing?' Granny said. 'The day after tomorrow when the cake is cold. Indeed we should have baked the cake a week ago but what could we do? Hannah, run and do your homework. We'll finish cleaning up here, Mark and I. Ben, I don't want your teacher telling me I'm neglecting you.'

'Ben, some of the girls in my class are going to a hotel for lunch on Sunday,' Hannah said when they were settled with their books spread out on the dining room table.

'Yeah,' Ben said. 'In my class too. But who needs it?'

Hannah gave up, but as she was lying in bed with her eyes closed, the picture of a television restaurant rolled up against her eyelids. Her last thoughts were that the people annoyingly never managed to eat their meal.

In the boys' room Ben had carefully shifted Mark's feet off his (Ben's) pillow and arranged him under the bed-clothes on his own side of the bed. They were not used to a double bed. Ben did not want to waken Mark because he was going to eat a bar of chocolate. He loved chocolate. At home his mother bought it for certain times and then made sure they washed their teeth. But of course Granny didn't know of that necessity. So Ben bought a bar or two each week out of his pocket money and ate it in guilty secrecy. He wasn't greedy. He would have shared but he guessed Hannah would say he should not eat sweets in Lent. Bed was not an ideal place for chocolate so after he had finished, he checked the sheets for scraps that would melt and spread. He wondered what to do with the wrapper. He knew a boy in his class who smoked cigarettes and was found out because he threw the butts under his mother's old-fashioned bath that stood on claw-feet. Granny's bath was a new one anyway from a couple of years back when her house and hundreds of others were renovated. He slipped out of bed and opened the window wider to throw out the blue paper and the gold foil. It was beginning to rain — big heavy drops.

At the first glimmer of light in the east the female magpie was agitating. 'I'm wet. I'm drenched. I'm saturated,' she clacked. 'This nest is hopeless. It's supposed to have a fine domed roof. All it has is holes. I'm a most bedraggled magpie.'

'You're a most be-maggled dragpie,' her mate cackled and swooped six times round the dripping tree, congratulating himself on his joke.

'It's not funny.'

'It's runny! Do you get it? The water, the rain. It's not funny, it's runny.' He was in great glee.

'Oh grow up,' she croaked. 'I'll have eggs any day. Five lovely eggs like last time maybe. All green and brown. I can't mind them in the wet.' She was worried. 'Go and find something to keep out the rain.'

In the murk of the early hour there wasn't much to be seen, but under Ben's window glinted the gold foil. He flew down and walked up to it cautiously, his wet back glistening. It was an ungainly walk, not graceful like his flight. He tweaked the cover carefully with his bill and the water ran off it. 'Just right,' he clacked. 'Waterproof. This'll be fine for poor old Mags.'

Together they poked the foil into the holes in their domed roof and smeared earth on the joins. Then the female settled in broodily. 'You never sing a song now,' she said in a quiet gurgly voice.

'I haven't sung a song for years,' he said. 'I'm growing old.'

CHAPTER 11

B Y FRIDAY THE CAKE WAS COOKED and cooled. The top was flat and glossy as it should be. Granny was flustered because Daddy would arrive on Saturday and she didn't feel the real preparations had been made. The bread bin was only half full and there were empty cake tins.

'We'll do our shopping with Mrs McGovern tomorrow,' Hannah consoled her, 'and I'll bake brown bread as soon as we come home. My bread is better fresh, it's not as good as yours.'

'Right so,' Granny agreed. 'Will you weigh the almonds and sugar or will we wait for the two boys?'

'We'd better wait,' Hannah said. 'I'll change out of my uniform. I've the kettle on for your tea and then they'll be home.'

When she was upstairs she could hear Granny still fussing. For a minute Hannah wished she could throw herself on her bed and read a book. It was weeks since she'd read anything but schoolwork. Friday evenings were not as they used to be when Mammy was at home.

'A pound of ground almonds,' Granny said, 'and of course we have to weigh these because the packets are in grams and I will always think of them in pounds and ounces. Half a pound of icing sugar and half a pound of caster sugar.'

Hannah mixed them while Granny sipped her tea. Ben and Mark were drinking milk and eating biscuits. 'We use just the yolks of the eggs,' Granny said. 'Can you separate the yolks from the whites, Hannah?'

'Of course,' Hannah said, hoping the yolks would not break.

'I'll make meringues with the whites, can I?' Ben asked. 'Two egg whites, four ounces of caster sugar. We could buy cream tomorrow. We love meringues.'

Hannah stirred in the beaten egg yolks and lemon juice and a little sherry. There seemed to be a lot of paste.

'Do I put all this on? Do I roll it out first?' she asked.

'Only half,' Granny said. 'And we're supposed to roll it out but we won't. Put the half in a ball on top and flatten it out with your hand. It's clean, isn't it, just as clean as the rolling pin?'

Hannah pressed it out as well as she could. She thought it should be smoother and more even but Granny said it was grand.

'How about the rest?' she asked.

'Oh you roll it up in eleven little balls on top. They are the apostles,' Granny said.

'There are twelve apostles,' Ben said, as he rested for a moment from whisking the egg whites.

'We leave Judas out,' Granny said.

'He wasn't gone until Good Friday,' Ben argued. 'It's three weeks until that.'

'I suppose the eleven come from the Simnel cake being for Easter. Will we make it twelve?' Granny asked. 'Will we put Judas on with the rest?'

Hannah was finding it not so easy to roll the little balls the same size and make them look orderly on top of the cake. 'No,' she said. 'We'll leave him off. I don't like his face.'

'How would you know his face?' Ben demanded.

'There is a picture in our classroom now, a print showing Judas and Roman soldiers in armour. It's by Caravaggio, it's in the Art Gallery in Dublin,' Hannah said.

'Yes we know about that. It was discovered. We read about it in the paper,' Ben said. 'And there's another picture I heard about, of Judas on a wee island in the middle of the Atlantic all by himself. St Brendan faces up to him on his trip to America. A boy called Brendan in my class told the teacher about it.'

'And what happened?' Hannah asked. 'What happened when St Brendan met Judas?'

'I don't know,' Ben said impatiently. 'It's a picture, not a story.'

'Well, I don't like the look of Judas,' Hannah said.

'You're not supposed to,' Ben said. 'He was an informer.'

'Informers get killed,' Mark said and Granny looked quite startled.

'If he hadn't committed suicide would the others have killed him?' Ben wondered.

'Oh children, children,' Granny said, distressed. All three turned to look at her in surprise and then concentrated on their jobs. Eleven marzipan balls were settled round the top of the cake and Granny lit the grill to toast the top to a biscuit brown with an aroma that made them all hungry. The meringues were cooking in a very low oven.

'I'm going to ring for an extra large pizza,' Granny said. 'It's a thing I've often wanted to do. You children can advise me on what to order. You have all worked very hard. The cake is lovely and Ben's meringues will be beautiful in a couple of hours. You are very good children as I shall tell your father tomorrow and even though I've done nothing I'm quite tired.'

CHAPTER 12

On Saturday morning, Hannah slipped down to put Ben's birthday card in the hall. With buying a card and stamp for her mother she thought there was no sense in posting Ben's. The post had not come – there is a Saturday post in Belfast. She hoped Ben would get cards. He wasn't getting a birthday cake with the business of the Simnel cake. She hoped her father would bring a present with him but she did not count on it. He was coming to visit Granny, so he might not think of Ben's birthday. She had often noticed that he couldn't juggle attention the way her mother could. And of course his being away made a difference. 'Hannah,' she heard her grandmother call in a stage whisper. 'Are you up? Could you bring me a cup of tea?'

So she did and Granny sipped at it. 'I'd better get up soon, Hannah. There's a lot to do. Oliver will be here before we know where we are.'

'He won't be here until after four o'clock,' Hannah said, because Granny had told her that after her phone call. 'It's Ben's birthday, Granny.'

'Oh goodness, Hannah, isn't it well you reminded me. Look over there in my wee top drawer and you will find the card I bought him. But I haven't written it. Take my cup and find my biro.' Granny laughed at the terrible writing she did with her left hand and then she folded a five-pound note and put it in the envelope. 'He knows I couldn't go out to look for a present for him. He won't mind. He's a good boy, Ben, just like his father was. You are very lucky to have such a good father.'

'And mother,' Hannah added, taking the envelope to put it in the hall too. The post had arrived, two from the aunts in America and one from Mammy in Bristol. Grandfather in Cushendall never noticed birthdays now since Mammy's mother had died.

The rest of the morning was a rush of shopping, baking, having their lunch, lighting a fire in the sitting room because 'Your father is very fond of a fire'. Then they all hovered and hung about and looked out the front window to see if he was coming.

'He'll go into our house first. I know he will,' Ben said. 'He has to get the car and if there's any post there he will open it. And he'll go in and out of every room and into the garden to see if it's in order. He'll even maybe phone Mammy before he thinks of us.'

Hannah thought Ben was probably right and indeed he didn't arrive until nearly teatime. On Saturdays and Sundays they had their main meal in the middle of the day, or as Mark said, they had their dinner at lunchtime.

When Hannah saw her father opening Granny's gate, she thought for a moment that she would feel awkward greeting him. She hoped he would not mention her letter to him, since Granny was unaware of it. But when Granny opened the door Daddy put his arms round her and crushed her broken arm so that she gasped 'Oh' in pain. He stepped back in shock and the children laughed at him. So did Granny almost at once and he was saying, 'Amn't I a right idiot! Why didn't I watch myself? I never thought.' Then he turned back to the car to bring Granny a bunch

61

of flowers and Hannah took them off to put them in a jug.

'Ben, happy birthday,' he said then and Hannah was relieved.

'I hadn't time, Ben, to see about a real present for you. This is just a couple of tapes.'

'That's good,' Ben said. 'Because I want a maximum and minimum thermometer like the one here. I want to put it in our garden when we go home. Can I get one? I'm putting every day's temperature on graph paper.'

'That's great,' Daddy said. 'My old thermometer. Isn't that wonderful. You got him into that, I bet, Mother. You are a marvellous woman.'

'Hannah is doing stuff with Granny's charts,' Ben said to Daddy.

'Is that right?' Daddy said but he wasn't really listening. If Mammy had been there she would have said, 'Do you hear, Oliver?' and he would have said, 'Of course I do,' and would have begun listening then.

Mark, after staying at the kitchen door to begin with, was standing beside Daddy, leaning against his leg. After tea, Ben and Mark went upstairs to listen to the tapes and Hannah cleared the table. When she began to wash the dishes, Daddy got up and lifted the tea-towel to dry. He winked at Hannah and she smiled back.

In the morning he was at the door before Granny was dressed. Hannah and the two boys were ready to go to the church and Granny called that she'd be down in a minute.

'Your Mammy is a bit worried about you three,' Daddy said.

'Wait till she hears about Granny's broken arm,' Ben

said, laughing.

'But of course she knows about Granny's broken arm,' Daddy said.

'How?' they all demanded.

'We kept it a secret,' Ben said. 'We didn't want Mammy rushing home.'

'Oh you know your mother,' Daddy said, looking uncomfortable. 'She always gets to know things.'

'You told her,' Hannah said, but Granny appeared at the top of the stairs so they stopped and Daddy looked up to say, 'You are in great style this morning, Ma.' They got into the car and drove off.

At the church Daddy greeted all his former neighbours and Granny smiled proudly. She was happy that all five filed into one seat, with Mark staying next to Daddy. Hannah passed the leaflets since Granny's wrist prevented her. She even gave one to Mark though he could read very little. Now and again Hannah's mind wandered to the dinner they would cook. What time should she put the roast in the oven, or the potatoes to boil. And she must not forget the mushrooms as well as carrots and parsnips. For dessert Granny said that Daddy liked tinned pears and cream better than anything so that was what he was getting.

'Mammy never has that,' Hannah said. Mammy would despise such things.

'All the more reason that he'll get it here,' Granny said. So Hannah persuaded her to buy ice-cream for the children to go along with Ben's meringues. Now that Granny was stronger and more capable it was not easy for Hannah to know who was to decide what.

Daddy carved. He did at home too. But at home he

had an electric carving knife which, though noisy, made lovely thin slices. Granny's old carving knife, even after Daddy tried sharpening it, made chunks.

'I don't like thick meat,' Mark said but Ben kicked him and he kept quiet. Ben cut it smaller for him.

'Hannah had the idea of going to a restaurant,' Granny said, when they were all seated at the dining room table.

'This is far better,' Daddy said. 'Nobody can cook like you, Mother.' Hannah sniffed to herself. She was not very pleased with the meal. By the time she and Ben had served all in the dining room, the food was not as hot as Mammy always preferred. She had thought they should eat in the kitchen as usual but Granny insisted it was a special occasion. Well, she thought, if that's what they want, they have had it. She felt herself getting cross.

'Help me, Hannah, with the cake,' Granny said, rising from the table. She and Daddy were going to have coffee and the children Orangina. Hannah had already put the cake on Granny's best cakeplate with the gold curvy rim. But in the kitchen Granny produced eleven birthday candles and little coloured holders for them.

'I want your advice, Hannah,' Granny said. 'Will we put them in the almond balls or between them?'

'Oh between them,' Hannah said, laughing. 'We couldn't put them on top of the apostles. That would make it Whit Sunday.' She lit the candles and carried the illuminated cake ceremoniously into the dining room. Ben's face lit up. Mark shouted 'I want to help to blow them out.'

'It's Ben's birthday,' Daddy said but Ben nodded. 'Mark can help. There are so many.'

Granny put her good hand on Ben's shoulder. 'You are

64

a grand boy, Ben. They are great children, Oliver,' she said. They had to decide then how to cut the cake and Daddy managed that very neatly. Mark didn't like almond icing so Daddy ate his. Everybody liked the cake, especially since they had made it.

After lunch people came in to see Daddy and it was soon time for him to catch his plane back to London. 'Ring when you're safely back there,' Granny said. At the door Daddy gave each of them some money. 'For your extra expenses,' he said. 'And I'll see about your thermometer, Ben, in London.' Granny went up to bed for a nap although she came down to see the *Antiques Road Show* on the television as she usually did and said, 'It takes one antique to appreciate another,' laughing at herself.

It wasn't a bad day, Hannah thought, but not as good as looking forward to it. She still wished, as she scrubbed the roasting dish, that they had gone to a restaurant. And she had an uneasy feeling, which she tried to smother, about her mother's reaction to the news of Granny's fall.

'Great activity in the old woman's house,' the male magpie told his mate. He nodded his head towards the lighted window of the dining room. When he nodded his head in that direction, his tail tilted up towards the darkening mountain. 'Some good cake crumbs with icing down there. Not great feeding but tasty. Are you going down?'

She didn't answer. She sat on sleepily, her white breast sheltering her eggs.

'Not a word out of her,' he complained. 'The next few weeks aren't going to be great clack.' Then he saw a cat crossing McGovern's garden in the dusk, white and black

and amber. He dive-bombed it. It stopped and raised its head towards him, its eyes narrowed in the greatest contempt. He kept his distance and the cat went on its way, putting each paw down daintily.

'Clack-yack-yack,' the magpie shouted after it.

'Pussy-cat, pussy-cat where have you been?

Waiting to pounce on a thrush on the green!'

It wasn't much of a poem, he thought. He had a notion he had heard some of it before. And of course although there were grassy gardens and parks in Belfast there was nothing that people called 'the green'. 'Just as well that Mags has gone sleepy or she'd have mocked at me,' he croaked.

After the cat had disappeared, he watched crows descending on Lynchs' compost heap. They had found great stuff to eat, it was plain. He joined them. He could smell cheese. Crows love cheese.

He took a peck or two but the crows were carrying it away in sticky billfuls. He gathered a morsel for Mags.

'They're all stuffing their beaks down there,' he told her. 'Rooks, ravens and great corbie crows.'

'It's well you put a good roof over us or they'd be attacking us,' she said. He clacked, congratulating himself.

She tasted it. 'Hmm,' she said. 'A cheese soufflé that collapsed. A very good flavour.'

They ate it together as the lights went on in windows up and down the road.

CHAPTER 13

A FTER TEA HANNAH WENT into the dining room. Ben and Mark had put the tablecloth and napkins into the washing machine, hoovered the floor and straightened the chairs round the table. So Hannah was able to lay out her homework. She put her mind to it and finished all expeditiously. First she re-did the graph for 21 March because it is easier to re-do something than to begin new writing. She discovered that the average maximum temperature over the twenty years for that day was 9.6 degrees celsius and that there was no upward or downward trend. The minimum temperatures varied between minus 2 and plus 7. The average was 2.6. There was no obvious trend there either. She didn't think she had found out anything but she had written it neatly, and she could do the other dates before the next geography class.

Miss Sterling looked at it and asked why she had chosen those dates.

'One for each season,' Hannah said, thinking it was plain to be seen. She had raised her eyebrows as she said it but she was unaware of that.

'But those particular days - 21, 20, 8, 30,' Miss Sterling persisted, turning from graph to graph.

Hannah blushed. 'Well the 21 March is one brother's birthday and 8 September is another.'

'I see,' Miss Sterling said. 'So you're not the dry-as-dust scientist after all.'

Hannah was raging. Who ever said she was, and why

should scientists be described as dry-as-dust? After the class was over, her friends rallied round, agreeing with her that Miss Sterling was awful and that they all hated her, so that Hannah began to think maybe she wasn't as bad as all that. She told Granny about it as she would have told her mother. Once she had it off her chest, it no longer hurt.

'I'm surprised at her,' Granny said. 'How does she expect girls to take up science and see the wonder of it if she talks like that?'

Hannah was pleased.

'Maybe I'll be a meteorologist,' she said.

'Or a geologist,' Granny said. 'I always wanted your father or one of the girls to study geology. Your grandfather used to show them all the types of rocks and raised beaches and other marks of the ice sheet. It was part of every holiday.' Granny was beginning to look as she did before she broke her wrist. She had a good pink and white colour again.

That evening, when Mammy rang, Hannah and Ben listened to Granny answering questions about her arm and her health. Granny handed the phone to Hannah, whose heart was thumping, and left her alone.

'Hannah,' her mother said, 'it was quite wrong of you to hide Granny's accident from Daddy and me.'

Hannah said nothing. She was surprised at the stern tone of her mother's voice.

'What would you have done if Granny had not recovered so well?' the voice went on.

'We wanted to prevent you from rushing home and losing your chance on the course,' Hannah protested.

'Children should not take it on themselves to protect

their parents,' her mother said. 'If you had told Oliver or me, we could have made up our own minds what was best. That was the right thing to do, not go thinking you were capable of dealing with everything on your own.'

'But we were capable,' Hannah said in triumph. 'Granny is nearly better and we are fine.'

'And your schoolwork?' Mammy said. 'How has it suffered?'

'Oh, not at all,' Hannah said. 'My coursework got great praise from Miss Sterling. Granny has charts and things that we don't have in our house. Ben and I have great ideas from them. And Mark's reading is improved from the children's books we found in the bottom of Granny's bookcase.'

Hannah was almost a teenager after all.

'I hope you didn't untidy Granny's rooms,' Mammy said.

'No, no. We fixed everything up after us. We're great housekeepers now. You won't know us when you come home.' Hannah felt she had won.

'And your clothes?' her mother went on. 'Your school blouses and the boys' shirts?'

'All spotless,' Hannah said. 'The washing machine washes them and I've been ironing for years and Ben too. You know that. Granny does some ironing with her left hand. She's very good with her left hand now.'

'Don't be ridiculous,' Mammy said. 'Anyway, I still mean what I said at the start. I am glad you managed well. But it was foolhardy. Your father and I would have worked it with less pain all round. However, no hard feelings I hope.'

'Not at all, why should there be?' Hannah said, her heartbeats choking her.

'I'm trusting you to tell Ben and Mark what I said. I don't want to have to say it all over again. I didn't enjoy saying it.' Hannah could feel her mother's heartbeats the same as her own. 'No hard feelings,' her mother repeated.

But there were. Indeed there were.

'She doesn't like me at all,' Hannah said to herself. 'I heard it in her voice. She thinks I'm horrible.'

She didn't quarrel with what her mother said. It was just the sound of her voice. How would she live the rest of her life if her mother disliked her? She knew some girls at school who were constantly telling of disagreements with their mothers. They didn't seem to mind. They seemed to relish talking about them. They enjoyed fighting with their mothers. Hannah didn't want to join those girls. Hannah didn't want to fight with anyone. And mothers had to like their children. But the sound of her mother's voice rankled.

Granny was in the kitchen. The two boys were in the sitting room watching television. Hannah was afraid that if she began to tell what her mother had said, she would not be able to stop the tears. But she knew that Ben would want to know about the phone call.

'She said we should have told them straight away,' she said when Ben turned his head to ask the question.

'I told you. I told you,' Mark shouted but Ben gave him a shove.

'Was Mammy cross?' Ben asked.

'Yes,' was all Hannah said, not trusting her voice.

'Oh well. We did what we thought best. And we managed, didn't we. We're all right. Mammy got her course. Daddy got his dinner yesterday,' Ben shrugged in an exaggerated way, as he had been doing lately.

Hannah gathered her resources. 'If we had done what Mammy says, we would have rung Daddy. He would have rung Mammy because he can't leave his work. She would have come tearing home saying, "I can't leave home for five minutes." She would have thought us all great useless lumps and she would have banged pots around in the kitchen for the rest of the time.'

'She would not,' Mark shouted. 'Mammy doesn't bang pots.'

'She sure does,' Hannah said.

'It's you who bang things around when you're cross,' Mark cried and Ben took him by the arm.

'Leave it. Leave it. Come on Mark, upstairs. I'll hear your spelling and I'll read your story when you're in bed.'

When the boys were gone Granny came in and switched over to a school quiz on the television. After a while Granny said, 'Your mother has upset you,' and Hannah nodded. 'Strictly speaking,' Granny went on, 'your mother is right. It would have been wise to tell Oliver straight away when I fell but you saved them both a lot of anxiety and frustration. Your Daddy is thankful to you, I know. Your mother will come round.'

'She was really angry,' Hannah said. 'She was cross with me.'

Granny laughed. 'She was cross with me too.'

Hannah knew that her mother and her grandmother did not always see eye to eye although they tried to hide their differences, since they were both good women.

'Your mother prides herself,' Granny said, 'on knowing everything that is going on in her family.'

'So do I,' Hannah admitted.

'There you are!' Granny smiled. 'She thinks her sixth sense tells her all about her children's lives. Then here was this wonderful adventure going on, these great achievements and she hasn't a clue, not an inkling. Oliver rings me to tell me he's coming over, I tell him what has happened and he rings your mother straight away. He never could keep a secret, Oliver, nor his father before him. Your mother starts worrying. "Oh my poor chicka biddies! Are they starved, dirty, and in tears." She agonises all weekend until Oliver tells her you are all grand, so she loses her temper. You've seen women now and again in the shopping centre frantic because of a lost child and when he turns up she wallops him. Same thing, although your mother would not like the comparison.'

Hannah didn't really like the comparison either, picturing a red-faced two-year-old squalling and a tormented mother slapping his legs.

'You and Ben,' Granny went on, 'have grown up years in the past month. You have run the house. You have done your schoolwork. You have been very good to me. You have been polite to all my neighbours. They say what a delight you are – and Mark too of course. Many a wee boy would have been crying for his Mammy. Your mother is afraid she will find her children all changed when she comes home at Easter. She wanted to get you back the way she left you. But I'd say she's sorry now she was so sharp with you. She's saying to one of her friends what a marvellous girl you are, and what could have possessed her to speak to you in that way. She's wondering will she ring you or will she write you a note.'

'How do you know all this?' Hannah asked.

'I know everything,' Granny said. 'I'm just like your mother.'

'And me,' Hannah laughed, whereupon the phone rang and her mother said, 'Hannah, love, I'm sorry I was so cross, I wanted to say it before I went to bed.'

'It's all right,' Hannah said.

'I hope it is now,' Mammy said. 'I think you're a great girl. It's just I was worried about you all. But I was nasty. I am sorry. And I was cool with Granny too. Will you put her on so that I can apologise. Why don't I keep a check on myself! Goodnight now, love. Sleep tight. I can't wait for Easter till I see you all. I'll talk to Granny now.'

'I'll survive,' she heard Granny say on the phone, not very warmly. 'Yes, the children were upset. It was a bit of a rocket. Indeed they were very good. Yes, you were right to ring Hannah straight away. She would have been miserable otherwise.' Then Hannah thought she'd better shut the sitting room door and not be listening to grown-ups' conversations. As soon as Granny put the phone down Hannah ran upstairs to tell Ben while he was still awake that everything was all right. Mark was sound asleep.

'I knew it would blow over,' Ben said. 'Women exaggerate. They fuss. I just steer clear.' He put down his book on the floor beside the bed and Hannah turned off his lamp. 'Goodnight,' she said and so did he, his head burrowing into the pillow.

But when Hannah closed her eyes she had to try very hard to see her pink balloon on the gate at home. The string would not hold taut and the balloon was in danger of snagging on the hedge. There was no sun, no blue sky. She looked for her mother's smiling face but it sagged into a frown so that she kept her eyes open for fear of what she would see. She thought of the jagged points up and down of her temperature graph. She laughed then to herself and fell fast asleep.

CHAPTER 14

I N GEOGRAPHY CLASS, Miss Sterling returned Hannah's course-work and asked did she know how to get the average temperature for each month.

'Do you mean average maximum and average minimum?' Hannah asked. 'Or should I add maximum and minimum for each day and divide by two and do that for the whole month?' They decided on the daily average for the month of January to begin with. 'You are a very capable girl,' Miss Sterling said. 'Your work is excellent. We'll have something worthwhile out of this.'

'I might go wrong in the long tots,' Hannah laughed.

'You won't,' Miss Sterling said dismissively.

'She wants something to show off to the inspectors,' Hannah's friend Claire said after Miss Sterling had left the room. 'She'll have you doing big charts to put round the walls.'

'But my name will be on them,' Hannah said.

'Then you'll be able to show off too,' Claire laughed.

'Nobody will ever look at them,' Hannah said. 'They will grow tattered and dog-eared and sad on the walls.'

They both laughed and then the French teacher came in and talked of a trip to France during the Easter holidays next year. Excitement at the thought of it nearly burst Hannah's chest, but like her friends she pretended it was nothing wonderful — maybe even a bit of a bore.

'Granny, some of our class are going to stay in French houses around Easter next year. Will I be let go?' she said, as soon as she came into the kitchen. Granny was struggling to make brown bread. 'Would you like me to finish mixing that?' Hannah asked, watching Granny's left hand trying to do the work of two. 'I could, you know — even though my bread is not as good as yours or Mammy's.'

'No, I'll finish this if it kills me or ruins the bread,' Granny said, smiling. 'Your bread is lovely. I just want to be able to do these things again.' In the end she had to use her right hand too and when the bread was in the oven, she washed the dough off the bar of the plaster across the palm of her hand. 'Thank God this will be gone in nine days.' She dried her hands while Hannah cleared the table, getting some flour on her uniform.

'Go and change your clothes like a good girl,' Granny said, 'and of course you'll go to France.'

'It'll cost money,' Hannah said.

'Everything costs money,' Granny answered. 'But if it's anything to do with education your Daddy and Mammy will have the money, like most Belfast parents. Anyway you are a lucky girl.'

Hannah thought maybe she was a lucky girl in some ways. It would be better if her hair would sit well oftener and if her feet would stop growing so big. When she came downstairs she told Granny about the new plan for the temperatures and Granny promised to check her adding because anybody could make a mistake adding thirty or thirty-one figures.

'I can add very well,' Mark said, when he came in and heard the conversation, 'I never make a mistake. My head is very good at numbers.'

Granny told him he was a great boy.

'I know,' he said, eating a piece of cheese.

At dinnertime he asked, 'Would we be here if Mammy had come home when you fell?'

Ben was kicking him under the table for fear he would upset Hannah again, but Mark could see no reason to keep quiet.

'I don't suppose so,' Granny answered. 'I'm very glad you're here.'

'What would have been arranged?' Hannah asked, because she had been wondering about that.

'Well,' Granny thought. 'At the hospital, before I came away, they told me I could have a home help without paying a penny because of my age and living alone. But I told them I didn't live alone these days, that I had a great family to look after me.'

'So you didn't need us at all,' Ben said.

'Of course I did. I'm an awkward body — as you know. I can't stand people other than my family around the house. I'd hate to have a home help. It wouldn't matter if it was Darina Allen or St Teresa of Avila; I couldn't tolerate her in my house every day.'

'If Mammy had come home she'd have arranged for you to have the home help and we'd have gone back to our house,' Hannah said.

'That's it,' Granny said. 'And of course your mother would have brought me dainty dishes and seen that everything was in order. She'd have been very good to me, but I'd have missed six weeks of your company.'

'And Ben wouldn't have missed his football after school,' Mark said and Ben shouted at him. 'Shut up. Shut up. Shut up.'

'Where do you play?' Granny asked.

'In the schoolyard,' Ben answered.

'No, I mean what position? Your Daddy used to be a back,' Granny explained.

'In goal,' Ben said.

'He's a great stopper of balls. He's the best goalie,' Mark said and although Ben's face was red, he could not help smiling.

'I'm sorry about you missing the football,' Granny said. 'But that couldn't be helped. You'll soon be back in your own house nearer your school. You had to bring Mark here from school. Your mother and I realised that you had to give up your football and we are pleased that you never complained.'

'He's going to play for Antrim when he grows up,' Mark said.

'Your Daddy used to have that ambition too and now he's living and working in England,' Granny said sadly. When the table was cleared she said, 'I have homework to do and it will be very hard for me.'

'What is it?' Ben asked and Hannah wondered.

'I'll help you,' Mark offered.

'I haven't written to Miriam or Anne in America since I broke my wrist. Of course we've been talking on the telephone. But for Easter I want to write each a letter as I always do. So I'll sit here at the table. I have my writing paper and my envelopes and my biro. I'll do one letter today.'

They all laughed, watching her begin to write with her left hand because nobody in their family was left-handed. After the kitchen was cleared Hannah and Ben went off to see to their own homework and Mark stayed to encourage his grandmother. Her writing, he saw, was nearly as good as his.

CHAPTER 15

THE NEXT MORNING the sun was shining in a clear blue sky when Hannah wakened. When Ben went out with the old magnet to take the temperatures, a fresh breeze came in the back door. While the kettle was boiling Hannah ran down the garden to cut a bunch of daffodils for the kitchen. She knew Granny liked them to bloom outside but she picked those that had been knocked over by the heavy showers they'd had. She shook off the big cold drops and threw away a snail shell from a yellow trumpet. She shivered and then smiled to herself, thinking the real winter was over and she could look forward to turning up her face to a warm sun. A magpie was balancing on the roof of the greenhouse. Hannah wondered for a minute if he was watching her. But she was too late to bother about the birds' breakfast. Only Granny had time for that.

At lunchtime she sat in a sunny corner. 'I'm going to get a good tan this year,' she said.

'And freckles,' her red-haired friend Judy nodded.

'A sprinkling of gold dust,' Hannah said, to show that she was not a dried-up scientist.

'Big brown blobs,' Judy said, laughing, and then they looked forward to France in a year's time. Judy had already settled with her parents that she was going and Hannah knew she would not be deprived, especially with her mother anxious to make up for her unreasonable phone call.

'We'd better learn a lot of French before we go,' Judy

said.

'Oh, I suppose so,' Hannah answered casually.

'It's not just I suppose so,' Judy urged. 'My sister Ita was there two years ago and they were at a convent on the Loire. For their lunch they got this meat stuff nobody recognised. The nun told them it was *cervelle* and only for one girl knew that meant "brains" they might have eaten them.'

'But they might have been nice,' Hannah said.

'Brains! Nice!' Judy exclaimed.

'And did nobody eat it? Was the nun cross?' Hannah asked.

'Oh she said they were silly stupid girls,' Judy answered. 'But they might have got mad cow disease.'

'French cows aren't mad,' Hannah laughed and they ran in because the bell was ringing.

In class when she had finished her maths before most of the other girls, she thought of brains. 'I have brains,' she said to herself. 'My temperature graphs are good. I'll be able to learn a lot of French before next Easter. I can do whatever I put my mind to.'

'Well, Hannah, you're in great form,' Granny said, smiling, when she came into the kitchen.

'Full of the joys of spring,' Hannah laughed and suddenly the weight of all her cares about her mother and grandmother and father were lifted and she thought, 'I can cope with this too!'

'It's wonderful what a bit of sunshine can do,' Granny said. 'Do you know I sat out on the seat at the back at lunchtime today. I had to clean off the birds' dirt first though. I could feel the sun doing my bones good. Only a few days now until I get this plaster off. Then I'll clean windows and do all the things I've missed.'

'I'll clean the windows,' Hannah said, jumping up, but Granny stopped her.

'No, no, no, love,' she said. 'Leave them for me. I'm looking forward to it all.'

'I'll do these,' Hannah said, pointing to the kitchen windows. 'To let the sun in!' And she squirted window-cleaner on the glass and polished away with a J-cloth even though Granny said it wasn't the best thing for windows. Hannah didn't care. She was in charge, capable of anything that had to be done.

In the run-up to the holidays, housework was no bother, she answered everything in class, her weekend English was praised. The world was a grand place.

On the Wednesday before Easter the school closed at lunchtime. When Hannah came back to the house Granny was there with her plaster off looking very disheartened.

'Your plaster's gone. Aren't you glad!' Hannah said.

'I'm glad all right,' Granny said, 'but disappointed. Look at it.'

She held out her wrist. It was bluish-white and creased. It seemed thinner than it should be. 'It's so weak!' she complained. 'I have less strength than when it was in the plaster.'

'Don't worry,' Hannah said. 'It'll soon come strong and with the plaster gone from your hand you'll be able to put it in water and wash dishes and make bread. They don't need strength.'

Granny sighed. 'You're a great girl, Hannah. I don't know what I'll do when you go home on Saturday.' Hannah felt she had really been a bit cheeky so she surprised Granny by giving her a hug.

CHAPTER 16

THAT NIGHT WHEN MAMMY RANG, Granny answered the phone, still lifting it with her left hand. Hannah heard the warmth ebb from her grandmother's voice in the short answers she gave. 'Of course you must do as you think fit . . . No, I don't mind in the slightest . . . All my grandchildren are welcome in this house. I have never said they were a trouble.'

Each sentence was frostier than the one before and Hannah began to wonder what was wrong — could her mother be taking a job in England leaving them with Granny? Had Mammy fallen out with them because of their behaviour or because of the way Hannah talked to her on the phone? Granny put down the phone without letting any of the children talk to their mother. She hadn't mentioned her visit to the hospital either, or her plaster removed.

'Well, Hannah,' she said coming into the kitchen. 'That was your mother.'

'Is she not coming home? What's wrong?' Hannah asked.

'Of course she is. Don't be ridiculous,' Granny answered crossly. 'She and Oliver are both coming home on Saturday as planned but they are not collecting you until Easter Sunday morning in time to drive us to the church.'

'Oh,' Hannah said, relieved that the chill was nothing more than that, but disappointed that she wouldn't be in her own home on Saturday night, wakening up in her own bed on Easter Sunday morning. 'I'd better tell Ben and Mark.'

'I should have thought any mother would be anxious to gather her children around her as soon as possible after being away for six weeks,' Granny said. 'But there, mothers are not the same nowadays.'

Hannah wisely said nothing. She thought to herself she could have felt insulted by both her mother and her grandmother, only there was no point. The two boys were playing dominoes with an old set they had found in Granny's bookcase. 'Mammy and Daddy aren't coming for us until Sunday morning,' Hannah said straight away.

'Oh, why?' Ben asked. Mark said nothing.

'Maybe they want to get the house fixed up before we all troop in,' she suggested. 'Or maybe Mammy is still offended because we left her out of what was happening.'

'Didn't you ask her?' Ben wanted to know.

'I wasn't talking to her. Only Granny. She wasn't a bit pleased. She put down the phone without giving it to me.'

'Why would Granny mind?' Ben wondered.

'I imagine she was looking forward to Saturday evening in a quiet house. She might have walked around all the empty rooms, thinking how good it was to have peace,' Hannah said.

'Goodness, I never thought of that,' Ben said. 'Does she really want rid of us? I thought she liked having us here.'

'A bit of both maybe,' Hannah said.

Mark pushed at Ben. 'Come on, Ben, it's your move, I'll soon have to go to bed.'

'Mark, do you hear that Mammy and Daddy aren't coming for us until Sunday morning?' Hannah insisted.

'I heard you. I heard you,' Mark shouted, throwing his

dominoes on the floor.

Holy Thursday was the first day of the Easter holidays. Had Hannah been at home she would have stayed in bed dozing or reading a book until she felt like getting up. So would Ben and Mark. Mammy would have gone off to work without wakening them. At Granny's when the alarm went off at the usual time, Hannah thought she'd better get up and bring Granny her breakfast. Nothing had been said about that the night before. Nothing had been said about anything the night before. Granny had stayed tight-lipped and grim, only bidding the children a stiff 'goodnight'. Hannah was puzzled that Granny should mind so much. She thought it was partly disappointment with her wrist and annoyance that her mother on the phone had not remembered to ask about it.

When she came in the kitchen door, dressed in jeans and a sweatshirt, there was Granny with the table set, the kettle nearly boiling and the smell of toast.

'Good morning, Hannah,' she said without turning round. 'I just thought, since I'm not a crock any longer, I'd get you out to school in an orderly way.'

'But we're not going to school,' Hannah said.

'What did you say?' Granny asked, buttering toast.

'The schools are closed for the Easter holiday,' Hannah said and Granny turned to look at her.

'Of course,' she said. 'My head is an old crock, never mind my arm.'

'Can I tell the two boys they may stay in bed?' Hannah asked carefully. She had heard no sound from their room.

'Yes of course,' Granny said, looking a bit confused. She had made quite a pile of toast.

'I could bring up toast and milk on a tray,' Hannah suggested. 'And Ben would hoover all the crumbs afterwards.'

'If I hadn't been in such a temper last night,' Granny said, 'I wouldn't have made such a fool of myself this morning.'

Hannah was glad to escape with the boys' breakfast tray. She was embarrassed. She warned her brothers to be sure and make no mess and to be specially careful with the milk. 'Granny is in a bit of a state,' she said. 'And we're not going to school so we'll be in her way all day. We'd better be no trouble at all.'

Downstairs, Granny had poured the tea but she hadn't touched her breakfast. 'Hannah,' she said. 'I must apologise for my bad temper last night. I don't want you to think I have any objection to you staying on a day longer. I don't like to be taken for granted but that is just my pride. However, I had been looking forward to going to the church for the Easter Vigil on Saturday night. I have always gone. I used to go to Tenebrae when I was young and when that was replaced by the evening triduum I never missed a single year. And now, of course I can't leave you children in the house by yourselves. But I'd be better to stay at home cheerfully.'

'We'll all go. Of course we will,' Hannah said. 'Mark didn't go last year because he was too small but Mammy said he would be big enough by now.' She wasn't a bit sure Mammy had said anything of the sort. But she thought that if they made him have a rest in the afternoon, he'd survive.

Hannah herself would not have wanted to miss any of

the church services in the days running up to Easter. This year on Holy Thursday, she appreciated the exact orders for the Passover, with the roast lamb and bitter herbs. She wondered what they were. Would mint count as a bitter herb or rosemary? She craned her neck, as everybody did, to see the people chosen to have their feet washed at the altar. Granny had said she always puzzled how the women managed with their tights. It was easy for the men to pull off a shoe and sock. Hannah loved the extra flowers that day and the candles and the singing. She appreciated the contrast on Good Friday with the stripped altar and the stark readings, and the cross.

On the way back to the house on Friday Mark was holding Granny's left hand and telling her all the things he was going to show Mammy when she came home tomorrow.

'On Sunday, Mark,' Hannah said.

'Saturday! Saturday!' he repeated. 'She was always coming home on Easter Saturday.'

'But I told you before,' Hannah said 'We're not to see them until Easter Sunday. They're calling for us to bring us to the church and then we'll go to our house for our lunch.'

'I've told him over and over,' Ben said quietly.

'I know you said that,' Mark nodded. 'But it's not true. Mammy wouldn't wait to see us. She'd want us first thing.'

'Don't be a baby, Mark,' Ben told him and he shouted that he wasn't a baby and pulled his hand away from Granny. In spite of her apology on Thursday morning she said nothing to help matters.

'If you don't stop acting like an infant you won't be

allowed to come with us on Saturday night,' Ben said. 'You won't see the bonfire outside and the church all dark until we light our tapers.'

Hannah hoped he wouldn't be disappointed. But he was very excited when the cold wind blew sparks from the wood fire and he clutched his taper so hard it bent over. There was a baby called Damian to be baptised at the altar and exultant alleluias sung by everybody before they went home. Mark's cheeks were rosy but his eyes were very sleepy in spite of the hour he'd spent in bed in the afternoon. Ben helped him wash his face, hands and teeth and he was asleep before his head hit the pillow.

On Easter Sunday morning a pink object bobbed among the hedges behind Granny's road.

'Is that the sun dancing?' the hen magpie asked sleepily. Her mate never knew if she was making fun or in earnest. He took a turn about the tree and said nothing.

'I heard that the sun dances on Easter Sunday morning,' she said. Then she poked her head out of the nest. 'It's a balloon,' she clacked. 'A pink balloon.'

'Will I burst it?' He swooped over to look at it and returned. 'I could, you know.'

'Of course you could,' she said scornfully. 'That big bill of yours could put an end to its dance, at one fell swoop. But why would you? We can't eat it. I think it's connected in some way to that worried wee girl you were watching in Agnews' garden.'

'Why is she a worried wee girl?' he asked.

'I don't know.' She shook her head. 'Maybe she's not worried any more. Maybe all wee girls her age are

worried.'

'I heard her singing yesterday,' he said. 'She's not a great singer but she's better than us nowadays.'

'Oh listen!' she fussed. 'Listen! I feel an egg beginning to break. Listen to the wee taps. Oh run and find some food for our lovely gawky little birds. This is better than the sun dancing and far better than pink balloons.'

CHAPTER 17

ON EASTER SUNDAY MORNING Hannah wakened early. She heard the magpies in a fuss out the back. She would have liked to jump out of bed and start scrubbing herself and Mark and even Ben to make sure they all looked perfect in Mammy's critical eye. But they needed their sleep if they weren't to be pale and cranky and have Mammy think they were not well looked after. Hannah told herself she would know if that was the way Mammy was thinking even though she would say nothing.

However, they were turned out to perfection long before the car stopped at the gate, blowing the horn. For the previous ten minutes Granny had been forecasting that they were going to be late for the first time in their lives. The Agnews, she said, were never late and she wondered what Oliver's father in heaven would be thinking of Oliver leaving his mother to the last minute to get to the church on Easter Sunday when they could easily have walked if he hadn't promised to bring them. She had been dividing her time between the front door and the front window but she had decided to ring up to find out what was keeping them when the horn blew. Mark dashed down the short path, nearly knocking Mammy off her feet as she stood out of her place in the front seat so that Granny could have it. She hugged him and hugged him, laughing over his head at Hannah and Ben. Granny was escorted into the front seat and Mammy and the three children squashed into the back.

It was practically noon by the time they had wished a happy Easter to their friends and neighbours outside the church afterwards. They stopped off at Granny's house because Mammy said they were all to use the bathroom.

'Is the water cut off at our house?' Ben asked for a joke.

'We're not going to our house yet,' Mammy said. 'When I saw you all looking so beautiful and grown-up I thought we'd bring you out for Sunday lunch. And what better place to bring you than to a castle.'

'A castle!' Mark shouted. He hadn't spoken much since his parents appeared so his voice came out loudly. 'Like in a story?'

'Or in a ruin,' Ben said, and laughed.

'Neither,' Mammy said. 'Belfast Castle used to be a big house for some lord a hundred years ago and now it has a restaurant. When Oliver mentioned that Hannah was hankering for a Sunday lunch in a hotel, we decided we'd go there. We booked it a week ago.'

Hannah beamed her happiness. This was a sure proof that her mother was friends with her again long before she arrived home.

'When will we get our Easter eggs?' Mark asked.

Daddy laughed and lifted him up. 'That's the boy!' he said. 'Always keep an eye on the essentials.'

'Would you like a cup of tea?' Granny said politely, as if they were strangers.

'Oh not at all,' Daddy said while Mammy was saying, 'I'd just love a cup of tea.'

'And undo the good of the bathroom,' Daddy said, so that Ben and Mark laughed.

'I'll make the tea,' Hannah said. 'Will I bring it here on

a tray?' They were seated in state in the sitting room.

'On the best china,' Daddy said, making fun again, and Granny smiled at last.

'Maybe just the three women will have tea,' Mammy said. 'And if Granny will permit, we'll have it in peace in the kitchen.'

Hannah prepared everything but she thought she'd better ask Granny to wet the tea even though Hannah had done that every day. It would acknowledge that Granny was the hostess.

'Now that your plaster is off, Granny, would you like to wet the tea?' she said, standing in the doorway of the sitting room. She saw the horrified guilt on her parents' faces.

'Goodness!' Mammy said. 'What can you think of us! We never inquired about your arm.'

'Well you never saw the plaster on, so naturally you didn't notice it was off,' Granny smiled. 'But Oliver is more to blame.' She pressed her good hand down on his shoulder as she passed his chair on her way out of the room. Mammy hurried after her.

'Look at your spotless kitchen,' Mammy said. 'And the children so well looked after. How did you manage it all?'

'I had help from three very good children,' Granny said. 'And Hannah is a jewel beyond price.' Hannah blushed.

The tea made them relax a little although Hannah could feel a strained note in the way they laughed too much at Mark, who kept on asking when he'd get his Easter eggs.

'They're waiting for you at home,' Mammy said. 'We didn't want them to spoil your lunch.' Then she turned to Granny. 'He wants the eggs but he doesn't eat more than little bits. Last year I found a great big lump of chocolate egg behind the couch in the living room. Ben likes chocolate though, don't you Ben?' She smiled at him and Hannah wondered why he grew pink. She didn't know about the nights he ate pieces of chocolate bars in bed, not really enjoying it because it was a secret.

'When are we going to this castle then?' Mark said, so Hannah and her mother washed up and left everything tidy in spite of Granny's protests that she'd have all the time in the world to do such things when she came back. They drove down the familiar Falls Road and up the unfamiliar Antrim Road with the Cave Hill on the left and Belfast Lough on the right and the sun glinting on the water.

'I haven't been up here for years and years,' Granny said. 'I used to have cousins living on the Cavehill Road. I came to visit them on Easter Tuesday in 1941.'

'You are going back,' Daddy laughed.

'I was young,' Granny said. 'Very young. It was a day like today with bright sunshine but by evening the sky was gone pink. It was a bit cold and all up around the hills were these giant balloons, barrage balloons they were called. They were silver but that evening they were deep pink, especially the ones over the hill here with the reflection of the sunset over Divis.'

'Were they for ornament?' Hannah asked, puzzled.

'What?' Granny said, her mind in the past. 'Oh not at all, Hannah. There was a war on. They were put there to keep out bombers, planes I mean. They were supposed to keep Belfast safe.' She gave a bit of a laugh.

'And did they?' Ben asked. Hannah knew from her history that they didn't.

'Indeed no,' Granny said. 'That very night, 16 April 1941, the bombers came over in force and half the town was wrecked and hundreds of people were killed.'

'Were you frightened, Granny?' Hannah asked.

'Terrified,' Granny said. 'They didn't come near our part of the town because we were furthest from the docks and the factories but the noise of the planes made us think they were overhead and the explosions and the fires were dreadful.'

'How about your cousins?' Hannah asked.

'Their house was damaged so they went back to the country. We lost touch with them,' Granny said.

'Oh Mother,' Daddy said. 'Cheer up. We don't want to be reminded of Belfast's troubles in the past.'

'You're quite right,' Granny said. 'We've a lovely day now, thank God'

They drove up the avenue to the Castle and parked the car alongside others. People were arriving in droves and standing round admiring the view over the Lough to Bangor and the little County Down hills. Ben had gone over to inspect the squat black cannons at the door.

'Do you think these were ever used, Daddy?' Ben asked. 'What are they here for?'

'I think they're here to pretend it is really an old castle,' Daddy said. 'I imagine they'd be about as useful as Granny's barrage balloons.'

Mark was shouting about big cats with green eyes down in the garden.

Hannah watched the way Granny looked so admiringly at Daddy while he smiled at Mammy and Mammy took in each of her children with love. She cut loose her pink balloon. It hovered among the trees of the Castle grounds, in danger once or twice from sharp branches. Then it soared away up over the top of the Cave Hill, and the south wind carried it off in the blue sky towards the Glens and Cushendall, where it reminded a lonely man, walking his dog by the sea, that he had three fine grandchildren in Belfast.

Mammy took her arm. 'Come on, Hannah. In we go,' Mammy said. 'A table for six for the Agnew family. We are going to enjoy an Easter Sunday lunch in Belfast Castle.'